Berkley Prime Crime titles by Riley Adams

DELICIOUS AND SUSPICIOUS
FINGER LICKIN' DEAD
HICKORY SMOKED HOMICIDE
RUBBED OUT

RUBBED
OUT

Riley Adams

BERKLEY PRIME CRIME, NEW YORK

THE BERKLEY PUBLISHING GROUP
Published by the Penguin Group
Penguin Group (USA) Inc.
375 Hudson Street, New York, New York 10014, USA

USA | Canada | UK | Ireland | Australia | New Zealand | India | South Africa | China

Penguin Books Ltd., Registered Offices: 80 Strand, London WC2R 0RL, England
For more information about the Penguin Group, visit penguin.com.

RUBBED OUT

A Berkley Prime Crime Book / published by arrangement with the author

Berkley Prime Crime Books are published by The Berkley Publishing Group.
BERKLEY® PRIME CRIME and the PRIME CRIME logo
are trademarks of Penguin Group (USA) Inc.

For information, address: The Berkley Publishing Group,
a division of Penguin Group (USA) Inc.,
375 Hudson Street, New York, New York 10014.

ISBN: 978-0-425-25999-3

PUBLISHING HISTORY
Berkley Prime Crime mass-market edition / July 2013

PRINTED IN THE UNITED STATES OF AMERICA

10 9 8 7 6 5 4 3 2 1

Interior text design by Laura K. Corless.

To my family

Acknowledgments

Thanks to everyone who helped me research and write this book. Thanks especially to Neil Gallagher, pit master from the Too Sauced to Pork championship BBQ team, for giving me the lowdown on the workings of Memphis festivals. To my agent, Ellen Pepus, and editor, Adrienne Avila, for their invaluable support and help with the novel. Thanks to my family for their encouragement, love, and patience.

Chapter

1

"Lulu, I just want to string this guy up."

Lulu's friend Cherry was polishing off a barbeque plate and waving her fork around in the air to punctuate her tirade. They were sitting in great wooden rocking chairs on the front porch of Lulu's barbeque restaurant, Aunt Pat's, for what should have been a very relaxing lunch. But Cherry was wound up tighter than a top. Her plastic fuchsia and lime green bangles jangled on her wrist as she waved her arm around.

"And that's because you don't like the way this Reuben looks?" asked Lulu with a frown. "That doesn't really sound like you, Cherry."

"It's not just that. Well, I don't like his sneering grins, but that's not the only problem. It's his attitude. He acts like he's God's gift to barbeque. He's completely con-vinced that he's got this barbeque competition in the bag. That rascal struts around like he's this amazing cook and tells us we don't know what we're doing. Makes me so mad, I could spit. He rubs everyone the wrong way."

"Sounds like a real winner," said Lulu with a sigh.

Cherry said dejectedly, "Maybe he will be a winner. That's another big problem. He's a good cook, I hear. But he's so unbearable that I don't see how anybody could stomach the food and listen to his mouth at the same time. He's so ultracompetitive. The other folks that I know who entered the Rock and Ribs barbeque competition want to have fun, hang out with friends, and pig out on some great food. Winning a prize is really the last thing on their minds. This fella is all about the winning."

"Is the rest of his team just as bad, or are at least a few of the people in his booth okay?" asked Lulu, rocking gently as she listened.

Cherry licked a little onion ring off her fingers and said, "He's got a couple of teammates, but it looks to me like he does most of the work himself. And a lot of the bossing around himself. There's a man named Brody and his wife, Sharon. They seem irritated most of the time, but then they're hanging out with Reuben all day, so that could be why."

"Completely understandable," said Lulu.

"There were a couple of others who made up the rest

of the team at first, but Reuben was so impossible that they haven't been back. It doesn't really matter, though, since we're all Patio Porkers and aren't in the major competition. You only need a few people for the Patio Porkers since we're only cooking spare ribs and competing against other small booths."

"What a mess," said Lulu, shaking her head. "But I'm surprised to hear that you're letting him get to you. You're a fine cook and I'm sure the booth is as cute as it can be. Can you try to ignore him?"

"No. 'Cause he won't leave us alone," said Cherry grouchily. "If he'd just stay in his booth and stop popping over to ours, then we'd be fine and dandy. Every time he comes in our tent, he's criticizing something about the way we set up the grill or our decorations or whatever."

Lulu said, "Isn't that what they call trash-talking? I bet he's trying to get a rise out of you to keep you from focusing. He probably thinks that gives him an edge."

"I absolutely do not know. He's baiting me all the time, Lulu."

"Maybe he has a crush on you," said Lulu, hiding a smile.

Cherry rolled her eyes in a way that would have been the envy of any teen girl. "I doubt it. But whatever it is, it's driving me nuts. That's why I ran over here—I needed to escape before I did something I might've regretted."

Cherry attacked her onion rings with enthusiasm. "I

need some grease," she said, dipping a ring into the large puddle of ketchup on her plate. "Not that your onion rings are too greasy, Lulu. Actually, they're perfect. But you know what I mean. Grease is my coping mechanism when I get stressed out."

Lulu laughed. "Not that you ever get really stressed out. But I'm like you—food helps me deal with stress." Lulu looked ruefully down at her plump figure.

Although Lulu could tell that Cherry was stressed today, you couldn't really tell from her appearance. As usual, she wore cheerful neon-colored clothes that clashed with her henna-colored hair and large, jangling bracelets, and had her Elvis motorcycle helmet close beside her. Cherry claimed that life was too dangerous to face without a helmet.

Lulu, with her white hair demurely tucked into a bun and customary floral print dress, felt positively faded next to her.

"I do too get stressed out. At least once a week I endure stress during my docent gig at Graceland."

"Is it because of that little woman who keeps coming on the tours and messing with you?" asked Lulu.

Cherry gulped down a large forkful of onion rings and chased it down with some ice-cold sweet tea. "That's the one. I swear I don't know what that old lady's problem is. If she thinks I don't know anything about Elvis, then why does she purposefully get in my group for Graceland tours?"

"And why," wondered Lulu, "does she go to Grace-land every single day?"

Cherry blinked at Lulu. "That's not the surprising part, Lulu. She's paying homage to the King, that's all."

Naturally, Cherry wouldn't find anything odd about a daily trip to Elvis's home.

"I only wish that she'd stop interrupting me every single time I open my mouth. And I wish she'd stop chucking out obscure factoids about Elvis's life. Every-body in my tour group starts listening to her instead of me. It burns me up."

It sounded like the little woman was angling for a spot as a Graceland docent. Wasn't that almost exactly how Cherry ended up with her volunteer role there? And the rest of Cherry's Elvis-obsessed friends, known as the Graces?

"This morning, though, it was totally Rock and Ribs stress. At first I signed up for the barbeque competition because I thought it would be a lot of fun. I dragged Flo and Evelyn into it and we've been planning the booth for months. But now with this Reuben making catty com-ments about our team, he's making me feel all serious and competitive—which wasn't why I signed up." Cher-ry's face was almost comically dejected.

"Evelyn? Evelyn's not cooking, is she?" Lulu couldn't keep the concern from her voice. Flo and Evelyn were two of the other Graces. The Graces were her very best friends and regulars at Lulu's restaurant. They were the

King's biggest fans and Graceland's very first docents—which had earned them their nickname.

"Hush your mouth!" said Cherry, with a panicked expression. "Absolutely not, no ma'am, she certainly isn't. She's our sponsor, since she's Miss Moneybags, you know. She insisted on putting up almost all of the money for the decorations, entry fee, tee shirts, food, everything. But Evelyn wouldn't want to cook and we wouldn't let her, either. She's enjoying herself by hanging out at the booth, drinking, and being decorative. I'm the one who'll mostly be cooking, but Flo will help me out, too. And I thought you could help me, Lulu, which is why I'm here."

"But folks who are affiliated with restaurants can't participate," said Lulu.

"I don't need you to cook. I need you to show off," said Cherry. "Tonight is Friends and Family Night at the festival. Since this Reuben is so high and mighty, I thought I'd introduce him to my best friend, Lulu Taylor—proprietress of the legendary Aunt Pat's Barbeque restaurant. That ought to take him down a peg or two." Cherry gave a malevolent grin at the thought.

Lulu squinted doubtfully at her friend. "He's more likely to take it that you're cheating or something—that I'm helping you out with your recipe."

"Who cares?" scoffed Cherry. "At this point, I want to show him somebody who really knows how to cook barbeque. Take some air out of his sails."

"Of course I'll be there for you, Cherry. Besides, I can't wait to see your booth all decorated for the festival. Are y'all entered in the best booth contest?"

"We are. Of course, a lot of the booths are super elaborate. But I sort of like ours, just the same," said Cherry. "Especially since it's covered with Elvis stuff."

"Covered with Elvis stuff? Wasn't the theme this year Siberia or something? How could you get away with doing Elvis?"

"No, it wasn't Siberia. It was . . . well, hold on, I forgot." Cherry tilted her bright red head to the side as if the bit of information she was looking for in there might fall out the side. "Oh, I know! Slovakia. That's it. So we're supposed to celebrate Slovakia for the Rock and Ribs festival, but all that means is that we represent the honored country by decorating our booths with that theme."

Considering the Graces' love for all things Elvis, Lulu had to wonder how they'd managed to pull in the Slovakia theme at all.

Cherry quickly enlightened her. "So we put an Elvis dummy in an apron with the Slovak flag on it, put a map of Slovakia on the walls of the booth with the town names renamed stuff from Elvis songs . . . stuff like that. You'll love it."

"I knew the Graces would find a way to incorporate Elvis into their booth design," said Lulu, beaming.

"We had to use Elvis. Otherwise, the Graces' booth wouldn't make sense. Our team is called Don't Be Gruel.

We had a regular party last night while we set up. Evelyn brought some really expensive liquor, Flo brought beer, and we were laughing so hard we almost threw up. Think you can make it over tonight?"

"I'll pop out of Aunt Pat's by five. You know usually this is such a busy time for us—Rock and Ribs brings gobs of visitors to town. They're enjoying spring—seeing all the flowering dogwoods and the azaleas blooming. And, of course, they all want to visit Beale Street," said Lulu.

"And eat the best barbeque in Memphis!" said Cherry with an expansive gesture to the Aunt Pat's dining room.

Lulu laughed. "I couldn't ask for better PR. I should be paying you. Anyway, I never usually even make it over to Rock and Ribs because the restaurant always needs extra hands. But this time we were proactive and hired extra waitresses and busboys as temporary help to get us through."

"Maybe we can really spend some time hanging out together at the festival, then," said Cherry, sounding excited.

"Sure thing! Besides, Ella Beth and Coco are dying to go to the festival this year. Usually, they can't really make it over, either, since all the adults are working. So I'll take a break from the restaurant and support y'all's booth and take my grands around and keep an eye on Derrick, since he's wanting to go to the festival with his girlfriend this year," said Lulu. Derrick Knight was the teenage nephew of her daughter-in-law, Sara. And Sara and Ben had recently been appointed Derrick's guardians. Cherry snapped her fingers. "Glad you mentioned Derrick. I need to ask him a question real quick. Is he home from the high school yet?"

"Should be here any minute. But you'll have to catch him before he takes off again. I swear that boy is tough to grab ahold of these days—always running off to do something. You wait here on the porch and I'll grab the cookies from the kitchen—they should be cooled off by now. You know I always have an after-school snack for the kids," said Lulu. "And food should keep him around for a while."

Cherry yawned. "That's fine. You go find the cookies and I'll close my eyes for a second and join the Labs for a nap." The restaurant's two Labradors, B. B. and Elvis, were sound asleep, curled up with each other on the floor. "I guess we must have partied a lot harder last night than I thought. Plus, the sound of the ceiling fans is enough to make me drowsy." She was leaning back in one of the high-backed rocking chairs and shutting her eyes when Lulu left the porch for the restaurant's dining room.

When Lulu bustled back with a plate full of still-warm cookies, Derrick was thumping up the steps onto the porch with his big school backpack. Amazingly, Cherry slept right through the ruckus. Derrick started tiptoeing, and he and Lulu were quietly moving off the porch to the restaurant's dining room when Cherry's phone rang.

That was apparently the one sound that was guaranteed to wake her up. She jerked in the rocking chair, arms and legs flailing as she tried to get oriented and scrambled for her pocketbook. All her commotion woke up the sleeping Labrador retrievers on the porch. "Where are y'all sneaking off to?" she asked them with a mock glare. "I wanted to talk to Derrick. Hold on, let me grab this call."

Cherry hit a button on her phone. "Yep. What's that? I'm on it. No worries. Bye."

Somehow Lulu's phone conversations never seemed to be that short.

Cherry threw her phone back into her small straw purse and clapped her hands. "Okay! That was team member Evelyn making sure I had the team tee shirts under control. And of course I lied and said yes." She gave a hoarse laugh and looked intently at Derrick. "Derrick, I need your help."

Derrick dropped his backpack against the wall of the porch and sat down in one of the rockers with a handful of cookies. "Sure thing. I have a little while before I've got to go meet up with some people. What's up?"

"Tee shirts! I need you to design the tee shirts for our team. Those get judged, too, you know, so I'll make you an honorary member of the Graces. But I need you to somehow weave in Elvis and Serbia. Oh, and barbeque. The team name, Don't Be Gruel, should be on it, and the team names—with mine as pit master, of course. And I need the design in"—Cherry glanced at her rhinestone-encrusted watch—"an hour."

"Whaa?" Derrick had the startled expression of someone who'd had ice water thrown at him. Despite his tattoo-covered, pierced, tough exterior, he had a completely vulnerable and insecure interior.

"You can do it, can't you, Derrick?" Cherry pleaded. "I'll be in so much trouble if you can't. I told Flo and Evelyn that I'd take care of the tee shirts and then I totally forgot. I thought we'd decided on just wearing our Elvis and Priscilla costumes, but the girls want tee shirts, too. If you can sketch something out this hour, then I can run over to the graphic print shop and get them to make tees out of it before they close for the day."

Derrick blinked and a red flush crept up his neck, coloring in the tattoos that were climbing there. "Cherry, it's not that I don't want to, it's more like I don't know if I can. I'm not used to making logo-type stuff or big sketches. I don't even know anything about Serbia. Plus, there's somewhere I've got to be soon." He looked as if he didn't want to talk much about where that *somewhere* was. Teenagers could be real vague about where they went and who they saw there.

"Derrick, I promise this won't take too long. If it does, you can stop and I'll try to finish up your sketch."

Lulu said, "I thought you'd said it was Slovakia, Cherry."

"Shoot! You're right, Slovakia. Not Serbia," corrected Cherry.

"I bet Cherry has learned a whole bunch about Slovakia lately," said Lulu, giving Derrick a comforting pat. "Why don't y'all go back into the Aunt Pat's office and brainstorm? I'll bring more goodies and milk for fuel. A project like this requires more than cookies—I'll serve up pasta salad and corn muffins."

Derrick reluctantly followed Cherry into the restaurant, casting worried eyes at Lulu. His self-confidence had gradually started increasing since he'd moved in with Lulu's son and daughter-in-law, but it was taking time. He'd been failing in school and getting into scrapes with the law before moving to Memphis but had rapidly made a turnaround . . . in everything but self-esteem. Maybe having a series of little victories like having everyone excited over his art would help.

Lulu patted the Labs, who were falling back asleep, then walked through the restaurant to the Aunt Pat's kitchen. Her son, Ben, was cooking up a storm at the stove, and brown sugar, bacon, and onion were sending out a heavenly aroma. "Were we getting low on sides?" she asked, spotting baked beans, corn on the cob, and corn muffins all being concocted at once.

"Lots of side orders to go," said Ben, really hustling, but turning for a second to give his mother a grin. "Looks like it's going to be another big month of Rock and Ribs sales for us."

Lulu found the pasta salad in the fridge and put a generous amount in a serving bowl. "This festival puts everyone in the mood for eating barbeque."

"Which makes it the best festival in the world, naturally," said Ben. "It's the perfect setup for us. Thousands of visitors can't eat at the festival since the barbeque is there to be judged and the health codes prevent it from being sold. So they end up with a huge hankering for barbeque that's not exactly satisfied by the fried foods and sweets that the vendors sell."

"And we're the ones to make sure they get some barbeque," said Lulu with satisfaction as she poured a couple of glasses of milk. "Did you know that the Graces have their own booth this year?"

Ben was focused on mixing more corn muffin batter and grunted in response. But his wife, Sara, who helped wait tables, walked in and overheard Lulu. "I hope they take pictures because I have a feeling I'm going to be up to my eyeballs in customers at Aunt Pat's and won't be able to get over there. You're going to take Ella Beth and Coco this year, won't you, Lulu? They're about to bug me to death to go and hear the bands and eat a bunch of fair food."

Sara was a solid, large-boned woman with curly, strawberry-blond hair that swung below her shoulders. She appeared sturdy enough to withstand any amount of begging, but she was a softy at heart.

"As long as they wear play clothes," said Lulu doubtfully. "You know how rainy and muddy it gets this time of year. Little Miss Coco is too fond of her fancy clothes."

"I'll see what I can do," said Sara. "Maybe she can dress up her play clothes with costume jewelry or something. You know how Coco is about accessorizing."

Sara picked up a tray and checked it against an order. "Did Derrick come in yet?"

"He sure did. He might be sorry he did come in. Derrick got waylaid by Cherry, who asked him to come up with a tee shirt design for the Graces right on the spot." Lulu sighed and put corn muffins with the milk and the pasta salad on a big tray.

Sara's brows drew together in concern. "Uh-oh. That could either turn out well or really bomb. I doubt he even has time to do something like that to begin with. Every time I see Derrick lately, he's rushing out the door without really even telling me where he's going."

This was what Lulu had noticed, too, and it made a seed of worry sprout in Lulu's mind. Surely he wasn't getting involved with those bad friends of his again, was he? But she said confidently, "Derrick is a fine artist. I'm sure with the pressure that Cherry's applying and a little brainstorming, he'll come up with something great."

And he did. After a panicky hour involving downing many glasses of milk and lots of snack food and fairly constant praise from Cherry and Lulu, Derrick's tee shirt design was proclaimed a winner. Cherry researched the country on the office computer and found it was mountainous so Derrick deftly sketched out caricatures of several of the Graces, wearing hiking gear, heading up a mountain, and holding a Slovakian flag. As a sop to Cherry, her caricature was hand in hand with Elvis (the 1970s lounge-suit-wearing incarnation).

Derrick, by the end of the hour, was dotted with perspiration. He kept tweaking the sketch and the lettering until Cherry finally said, "That's it! That's perfect, Derrick. Stop fiddling with it. I'm taking it over to the graphic guy to get the shirts made." She practically ripped the paper from him and took off, waving over her shoulder. "Bye. Bless you, Derrick! You'll be richly rewarded for this . . . promise."

Derrick's reward was his utter relief that Cherry had gone. Lulu leaned over and gave him a hug. "Thanks for saving the day like that, sugar. I'm amazed at how well you performed under pressure. That design was the cutest thing I've ever seen! Bet you'll win a prize for the tee shirt competition."

Derrick stretched, joints popping as he did. "If I do win anything, it'll be a miracle. Everybody else probably worked on their tee shirt designs for at least a couple of weeks."

"Well, you know how sometimes judges like things that almost look hurried. I've seen modern art that I didn't know if it was right-side-up or upside-down. And it was supposed to be worth millions." Lulu shook her head at the mysteries of the art world. She paused and tried to delicately word her next sentence. She wanted to know why Derrick hadn't been around as much as he usually was, but she didn't want to sound nosy or suspicious, either. "You've been super busy lately, haven't you, sweetie? Do you think you'll have time to go to the festival? And if you go, who would you go with?"

Derrick grinned at her, which made her realize that she wasn't as subtle as she wanted to think. "Peaches and I are still going out, Granny Lulu, so I'll probably go to Rock and Ribs with her tomorrow. And I told the twins I'd walk them around some, too. They said they were hoping you could walk around with them some, too. They're dying to go." He glanced at his watch. "I've got to take off now or I'll be late. See you soon, Granny Lulu."

Lulu gave a relieved smile. If he was spending all his time with that cute Peaches and the twins, there was no way he could get into any trouble. Surely. After all, what could happen at the festival?

Chapter 2

The yearly festival was smack dab in the middle of the rainy season in Memphis. It wasn't just rain, either—it was more like flooding. This meant that there was a whole lot of mud on the festival grounds at Tom Lee Park. Despite the gray clouds and rain, Memphis was still beautiful with the springtime blooming of dogwoods, multicolored azaleas, and Bradford pear trees.

Lulu stood ankle deep in mud and wore a slicker covered with pigs as she surveyed the Graces' booth later that evening. Fortunately for her, her ankles were inside a pair of checkered rubber rain boots. Even with the rain, there were thousands of people in the park.

"At least the mud made it super easy to put the tent

poles in," said Evelyn in a chipper voice, nodding to the booth's structure.

"Not that you had anything to do with putting those poles in," grumbled Cherry. Her red hair made a shocking contrast to the hot pink poncho she was wearing.

Evelyn raised her carefully plucked eyebrows. "My, but you're the cranky one, Cherry. You're right, though. I didn't help much with the actual booth construction."

Flo shrugged. "We didn't ask you to, Evelyn. Giving us the financial backing was really enough."

Cherry was repentant. "I know. Ugh. Maybe it's the rain making me sour. Sorry I'm so grouchy. I'm shaking it off," said Cherry, repeating the phrase like a mantra several times in a row while literally shaking her hands in unison. Then she took a deep, soothing breath and said pleasantly, "What do you think of our tent, Lulu? Think we have a shot at winning the booth decorating contest?"

She had no idea how their booth ranked with the ones around her, but she knew that the women had had a lot of fun when they came up with it. Elvis and Slovakia were everywhere. There was the Slovak coat of arms and flag and an artistic rendition of Elvis hamming up for a picture in front of a Slovakian castle. "It's perfectly wonderful, y'all," said Lulu, hugging Cherry. "I feel like I'm touring Eastern Europe. Now remind me again how the contest works. What are y'all cooking?"

"We're not in the really *big* competition," said Flo. "We're one of the Patio Porkers teams. That means that we compete against the other Patio Porkers for the best ribs. If a team wins the smaller contest, then the next year the rules state that they have to be in the big competition. Then we're also entering other small contests like best booth and best tee shirt."

"And don't the tee shirts look great, Lulu? You'd think we spent weeks on them," said Cherry.

"They really do," said Lulu. "I'm pleased as punch! Derrick did a wonderful job and I love that the color of the shirts is blue instead of plain white."

"Blue was one of Elvis's favorite colors," said Cherry. "So of course we wanted to include it with our theme."

"Too bad the shirts are bound to lose," said a snarky deep voice behind them.

They turned around to see a short, balding man with dark eyes and a sneering smile.

"Like you have good enough taste to know what's great and what isn't," drawled Cherry with a roll of her eyes.

"Lulu," said Flo quickly, "this is Reuben Shaw, the pit master for the booth next to us." She turned to the man. "This is Lulu Taylor, owner of Aunt Pat's Barbeque." Flo patted her big hair nervously, although it was so rigorously sprayed, that there was never a strand out of place. The mention of the restaurant made the man relax his stance. A respectful expression passed across his features. "Nice restaurant. I've enjoyed a few meals there. Haven't eaten there for a while—I need to make another trip."

"I hope you will and that you'll enjoy it," said Lulu, trying as hard as she could to be gracious, even if her friends were being treated poorly by this man. Usually you could draw more flies with honey. "I'm taking the week off so that I can enjoy the barbeque competition and take my granddaughters to the festival. Usually I never really get to come here since the restaurant is so busy."

There looked to be the smallest crease of anxiety on Reuben's face. "You're not on this team, are you? Not on the Don't Be Gruel team. Because you're a pro and I'm sure that's completely against the rules."

"I'm certain it is," said Lulu placidly. "No, I'm simply a spectator, here to enjoy the festival like anyone else."

He seemed to relax again. "Let me show you our tee shirts," he said in a peremptory tone, putting a hand on Lulu's arm and pulling gently.

As he walked away from the Graces' tent, Lulu heard Cherry grumbling, "Like she'd even care about his dumb shirts. Considering it was family who designed the Graces' tee shirts. Stupid man."

Reuben's grip tightened on Lulu's arm. Apparently he wasn't wild about being called stupid.

Having seen the Graces' tent, Lulu could tell that more thought and work had gone into Reuben's. Reuben had used a pig theme and had really taken a serious approach to including Slovakia. Where the Graces had put sketches of castles, Reuben had an actual castle replica in his tent. Everything, in fact, looked very serious, including the cooking area. The Graces seemed to be preparing for a backyard cookout. Reuben had set up what resembled a miniature professional kitchen.

His team, though, didn't seem to be having as much fun as Cherry's team. While Reuben showed off their tee shirt to Lulu (which did seem to be something of a work of art), they looked sullenly on. There was a blond woman with her hair pulled back in a ponytail, who was wearing a good deal of eye makeup and who watched Reuben with complete disinterest, and a tall man leaning casually on the castle, appearing bored.

"This is Lulu Taylor," he said to the two. "Owner of Aunt Pat's restaurant."

The blond woman nodded but didn't respond, but the man seemed to summon up interest. "Great ribs! I went there for the first time last week because one of my co-workers said he'd grown up going to Aunt Pat's."

Lulu smiled at him. "Well, we've been around for a long time. It was my aunt's restaurant before I ended up running it."

He had a reminiscent expression on his face. "My friend says you're got the best ribs in Memphis. He goes back every few weeks as a matter of fact. Says eveything is almost exactly the same as it was when he was a kid. Something very comforting in that," he said thoughtfully. He leaned forward and stuck out a thin hand. "I'm Brody Jenson," he added.

Lulu shook his head. "So nice to meet you."

Reuben gestured to the blond woman with a sneer. "And that's Brody's wife, Sharon. The rude one in the corner."

She shot him a glare that could have fried eggs, then stared determinedly down at the floor. Sharon's blond hair was going dark at the roots, and she had tired eyes and deep grooves making unhappy parentheses at the corners of her mouth.

"Nice to meet you, Sharon," said Lulu. The attitudes in this booth were confusing. It was easy to imagine why the Graces weren't happy with Reuben, but it seemed like the members of his own team shouldn't have the same issue. After all, they were the ones who chose him as the pit master.

He didn't look to be any kinder to his crew than he was to the Graces, though. "See all this stuff around you—the decorations? I came up with everything. Everything. I designed it, I built it, I put it up. I'm a contractor, so that's the kind of thing I really excel at. And the rest of my team is just around to enjoy the party." He almost spat the words.

The tall man stood up straight and his eyes narrowed. "You've got selective memory loss, Reuben. I did all the research to come up with the design. And Sharon and I both helped move all the stuff into this booth."

Sharon gave a disdainful laugh. "Besides, if your stamp is on most of the stuff in the booth, Reuben, that's because you're so pigheaded that you won't listen to anybody else's ideas or accept that your idea might not be as good as someone else's." Her lip curled and made her pretty face momentarily unattractive.

"I've got a mind to walk right out on you," said Brody, still fuming. "Then what would you do without your help? Good luck juggling the ribs and the seasoning while you're cooking for the competition." The idea seemed to please him and a faint smile pulled at his mouth.

Reuben's face darkened. "You wouldn't do that, Brody." It sounded more like a threat than a promise.

"Wouldn't he?" asked Sharon. "You should try him. And me—because this is really the limit of what I can put up with."

Lulu murmured, "I should be getting back to my friends." No one glanced her way or seemed to notice her or hear her, so she hurried off into the darkness outside the brightly lit tent—and ran smack into someone who was standing right outside the booth.

"I'm so sorry!" she exclaimed. But the person was already gone.

"Granny Lulu, is it time to go yet?"

She was ordinarily a morning person, but after staying up late on Family and Friends night at Rock and Ribs, she was dragging this morning. Her twin granddaughters, though, apparently had no such problems waking up. Coco was dressed to the nines and Ella Beth's chin had a determined set to it that meant she was ready to take on and conquer her day.

"Sweetie, we'll head over to Tom Lee Park soon. Just give me a little while to get all my engines revving. Coco, honey, you shouldn't be wearing that outfit to the festival," said Lulu.

Coco peered down at her linen dress with the satin sash. "It's a nice dress, Granny Lulu."

Sometimes she did wonder where that child came from. "The dress is as pretty as you are, Coco, but I'm worried about what might happen to it, not whether it's in fashion. The festival is a huge mud pit, sweetie. And the rain is still coming down in buckets. You'd really please me if you'd put something else on. Your mama is coming by the restaurant to work in a few minutes—let me call her real quick and ask her to bring you play clothes."

Of course, Ben should have been able to see that Coco wasn't wearing appropriate clothing for Rock and Ribs when he dropped her off at the restaurant, but sometimes Lulu wondered if her son noticed much of anything that went on around him.

"Did y'all get enough to eat this morning? Does anybody want to top off their tank before we head to the festival? We'll be doing lots of walking, so no one needs an empty tummy," said Lulu.

Coco tilted her blond head in a considering way. "What's here to eat?"

"Well, we probably don't have time to cook anything," said Lulu. "It's getting close to lunchtime, so if you wanted corn muffins or barbeque, I know we've got some ready."

Ben joined them on the porch. He still didn't seem to notice that Coco was a bit too dressed up for the muddy festival.

"Has Sara gotten here yet?" he asked.

"Not yet. But she's bringing a change of clothes for Coco, so that might have taken her some extra time," said Lulu.

Ben nodded absently and fingered his mustache. He cherished his facial hair since the hair on the top of his head had been steadily disappearing over the past few years. He preferred to think of his hair loss as just an expanding forehead.

"We're trying to figure out a quick bite for Coco to eat," said Lulu.

"Barbeque," said Ben, confused as to why there was any question about a quick bite at the restaurant. "I've got a whole batch I cooked up."

Coco said, "Do we have anything else to eat?"

Ben frowned at his daughter. "What do you mean, anything else?"

Lulu said, "There's lots to eat, sweetie. Why not have a couple of corn muffins?"

"I made coleslaw. Or how about baked beans?" said Ben.

Coco shook her head. "I'm getting a little tired of all that."

"Are you wanting something to satisfy your sweet tooth?" asked Lulu. "Maybe some gingerbread with butter? Or homemade peppermint ice cream?"

You could have knocked her over with a feather when Coco shook her head again.

"No," said Coco slowly, "I want something real basic. Like a peanut butter sandwich."

"Peanut butter and jelly?" asked Ben, sounding out the words as if trying out a foreign language.

"No jelly," said Coco with a small sigh. "Only peanut butter."

Ben and Lulu stared at each other.

"We don't have any peanut butter at Aunt Pat's," said Lulu. "It's usually not something we carry here."

"And not anything we *have* to carry, either," said Ben stoutly, putting his hands on his hips. "This is a barbeque joint. Why would we have peanut butter here?"

"I can see Coco's point, though," mused Lulu. "Somehow I've simply never gotten tired of barbeque and all the fixings. But I guess it's possible to get worn out from eating ribs, fried pickles, and red beans and rice."

"Never!" said Ben.

"Maybe I'm not worn out with it," said Coco in a firm voice. "Maybe I just feel like peanut butter sometimes."

"Tell you what, sweetie," said Lulu, giving her a hug. "I'll put peanut butter on my list and I'll make sure to bring it back to put in the office cabinet, especially for you. In the meantime, how about I make you a pimento cheese sandwich on some sourdough bread? I made some up yesterday."

Soon Coco was connected with no-nonsense, mud-worthy clothes, and the girls and Lulu headed off to Tom Lee Park. The rain subsided and they were able to walk around the festival without getting soaked. It seemed like there were even more booths than ever before—each one carefully decorated and with Slovakia prominently featured. The festival pulsed with music and excitement. A mixture of savory aromas wafted through the air—spicy ribs mingling with onion rings and cotton candy. And there were wall-to-wall people, happily mucking through the mud to be there for the mouthwatering food and soul-stirring blues.

Ella Beth stopped and sniffed the air outside one booth. "That one. Let's go to that booth, Granny Lulu. Something smells wonderful!"

"Your nose knows! It sure does smell delicious. But the booths aren't open to the public, remember? Once we head over to the Graces' tent, we can get some ribs. The food that's being cooked up is for friends of the people in the booth and the judges."

Ella Beth's freckled face was disappointed, but she quickly got over it when Lulu offered to buy the girls their choice of fair food from one of the food vendors. It was truly amazing, she mused, how many things could be fried. And it was a really good thing that they didn't eat fair food every day or they'd all be as big as barns.

"Now that we've all gotten set up with food, y'all, let's head over and see the Graces' tent. I think you're going to like it."

Ella Beth squinted up at Lulu in a considering way. "I'm guessing that it's covered with Elvises. And food."

Coco chimed in, "It's got to have Elvises or else it wouldn't be right. I think they made an Elvis statue out of barbeque."

Ella Beth frowned at her. "That wouldn't work, Coco. It'd be a falling-down sloppy mess. But I bet they could make an Elvis out of corn muffin mix. Mmm. That would be good."

Coco said, "Maybe they could do an ice sculpture of Elvis."

Lulu beamed at her. "And lovely it would be, too. But you know how hot it is right now. It would be a skinny Elvis in seconds if they made any kind of ice sculpture."

As soon as they reached the Graces' tent, the women swooped down on the girls. "We knew there was a reason that the sun came out!" chortled Cherry, dressed up like an early seventies version of Elvis.

"Aren't y'all the cutest things," crooned Flo. "Come to have some barbeque?"

Even Evelyn languidly unfolded herself from the lounge chair she'd brought in and hurried over to hug Ella Beth and Coco.

"Well," said Lulu, "we weren't sure if y'all were cooking yet or if you had anything left over—you know. We didn't want to presume anything. So the girls finished up deep-fried candy bars from one of the food vendors."

The Graces were horrified.

"Honey," said Flo, "we're cooking about twenty-four hours a day right now for the next few days. We've got better food for y'all than deep-fried Ho-Hums or whatever you bought from a vendor."

Evelyn, who looked to be dressed up like Priscilla Presley, said, "And we're inviting all kinds of folks to come in and sample from us. You know how it has to be invitation-only to come into a booth, but we're having a hard time being selective so we've already invited a total of about twenty-five brand-new friends to hang out with us. If we're inviting strangers, we'll surely be inviting you, too!"

Lulu asked the girls, "Do y'all have any appetite at all left?"

Ella Beth said, "We've always got room for barbeque, Granny Lulu. You know that."

Coco drawled, "Well, sometimes maybe I don't. There's only so much barbeque a girl can have in a day, you know. But I want to try the Graces'."

Soon the girls were sitting in the little eating area in the back of the booth, happily exclaiming over the food while Lulu caught up with her friends near the grill.

There was whooping and hollering from the next-door booth. Lulu said, "Sounds like you're real close to the action here. Any more excitement from the booth next door?"

Evelyn flicked lint from her 1970s-era miniskirt. "Oh, honey, the excitement hasn't stopped. Although they sound like they're in a good mood right now. And I'm in a good mood because I'm thinking they're too tipsy to do any competitive cooking. The fact that they're also not fighting is a bonus. Those folks have fought the whole time. Maybe they've gotten into the alcohol and that's improving their moods."

It was a little distracting having Evelyn dressed as Priscilla. But not nearly as distracting as having Cherry dress as Elvis. Lulu missed whatever it was that Cherry said.

"I'm sorry, Cherry. What did you say?"

"I said that we shouldn't say anything about them not fighting. That'll jinx it," said Cherry. She had on a black jumpsuit with a big belt and sunglasses. Her trademark Elvis motorcycle helmet was close by. Somehow the red hair simply didn't go with the outfit. Her gaze sharpened. "Lulu, you're looking at my hair. You don't like the redheaded Elvis look, do you?"

"I think it's fine!"

Cherry sighed. "No, you don't. No one else likes it, either. It's just that my wig was getting way too hot and itchy, so I took it off. I might have to rethink this. Or put my helmet on."

A husky voice from outside the booth said, "You look amazing. But not as amazing as Priscilla."

Lulu raised her eyebrows as a gentleman who appeared to be in his late thirties wearing a sheepish grin and fashionably shaggy hair hovered at the edge of the tent. The one thing that stood out about him was the white stripe of hair that went right through the middle of his dark hair, giving him a skunk-like appearance.

"Oh, well, if you're giving compliments, then you really must join us," said Evelyn, scooting over to make room next to her on the sofa. "I'm Evelyn. Or Priscilla, if you like." She fluttered her false eyelashes at him in what was surprisingly beguiling.

"I'm John," he said, holding out his hand. "John Smith."

"Surely not," said Evelyn. "Are there really any actual John Smiths?"

"Mmm," said Flo. "It does have that assumed name sort of ring to it."

"I'll assure you," said John with a very bright grin, "I'm completely genuine. I'd bring my mama in to attest to it."

"Well then. Sounds like you're all right to me," said Evelyn. "I've always been partial to mama's boys."

Although something about the man just didn't ring true to Lulu. Not that she could put a finger on it.

"Going back to the wig subject, I'm amazed that it doesn't seem to be bothering Evelyn at all," said Flo, carefully drawn-on eyebrows arched. "She seems to be enjoying it."

Evelyn snorted. "This bouffant isn't a wig, y'all. It's my real hair." She carefully patted her chestnut-colored hair.

"No, it isn't!" said the women, shocked.

"It surely is," said Evelyn, putting her hands on her hips. "I had my salon to do it especially for the festival. My stylist cried when she teased my hair. She actually, really, truly cried."

"I guess she thought she was ruining your hair for good," drawled John, winking at Lulu.

"It's a good thing you don't have to tease your hair all the time," said Lulu slowly. "It'd damage it in no time flat."

The hair musings were cut short by a shriek from the booth next door. Even Ella Beth and Coco momentarily stopped their chewing.

"You *dawg*! You no-good scoundrel of a *dawg*!" came a shrill voice. Then came the sound of a huge amount of commotion that indicated some sort of a struggle. Instinctively, they ran over—Flo quickly volunteering to stay with the girls. Cherry grabbed a plaster Elvis—Lulu didn't know whether it was for luck or protection.

Chapter

3

Sharon was standing on a chair and giving high-pitched yells, almost like she'd seen a mouse. Brody had his hands around Reuben's neck and was giving every indication of not letting go.

They looked over at John, who'd run over with them, but he'd apparently quietly slipped away and it was only Cherry and Lulu. Lulu took a deep breath.

"Y'all, this is no way to handle a problem—you know that. Let's think of another way that we can work around this," said Lulu in as reasonable a tone as she could muster, considering the scene in front of her.

Brody said through gritted teeth, "He insulted Sharon. I'm protecting her honor."

"Well now," said Lulu in a determinedly cheerful

voice, "this should be easily fixed. Reuben, if he can talk with you squeezing his neck, can apologize. Then Sharon can tell Reuben that he's forgiven. And y'all can go back to cooking and having fun and enjoying this festival."

Reuben, oddly, seemed not really to be listening. He stared at something outside the booth. Sharon's voice quickly brought his wandering attention back, however.

"He's not forgiven," said Sharon with icy eyes. "Why would I forgive someone like him? Nasty, nasty man." Her voice started rising again as she got herself riled back up. Lulu sincerely hoped that Flo had taken the girls off for a stroll. "And don't be coming by our house anymore. We're done with you, Reuben Shaw!"

Reuben was somehow able to find his voice, although it didn't sound as strong as it usually did, considering how Brody's hands were clutching his neck like a vise. "Won't go to your house. Don't like it anyway."

This wasn't the effect that Lulu had been hoping for. Sharon apparently took offense that her home was being insulted.

"The very next time you do make your way to our house to pester us for one thing or another," hollered Sharon at the top of her considerable lungs, "I'll kill you!"

Reuben made a sudden move and pulled away from Brody to lunge at Sharon, who shrieked more and jumped over to a tabletop. At this point, Cherry jumped into action. She hefted the plaster Elvis and hit it hard against Reuben's head.

Reuben stumbled and quickly sat down on the booth floor, looking dazed. That was when Pink Rogers, a Memphis police officer and friend of Lulu's and the Graces', entered the booth. He gawked at the sight of the blond woman on a tabletop, the stunned man on the floor, and Cherry holding the remnants of an Elvis. He quickly straightened up to his full and imposing six-feet-seven-inch height. "All right. What's going on here? What's all the shouting and . . . hitting? Cherry?"

Cherry's mouth comically flapped open and closed a few times.

Pink sighed and caught Lulu's eyes. "Lulu? I'm sure you can explain this all to me or make sense of all of this."

"We heard a lot of commotion in here while we were visiting next door, Pink. We rushed over and saw that these folks were all having . . . a disagreement," said Lulu slowly.

"A lively one, I'm guessing," asked Pink grimly.

"You might say so, yes," said Lulu, smoothing down her floral dress.

"I was trying to prevent that Reuben—that weasel of a man there—from attacking Sharon," said Cherry, still flushed with anger.

"It looks like y'all have been really going through some beer here," said Pink, nodding his head at a bucket full of empty bottles. "I need you to calm down, pull your heads together, and stop acting out. If I have to come back here to arrest somebody, I won't exactly be tickled pink, you hear?"

Sharon and Brody nodded, staring at the floor, but Reuben seemed hardly to be listening again.

Pink stared at Reuben through narrowed eyes. "Look, fella, I'm talking to you, too. You seem to be at the bottom of all this. I need to hear that you're going to turn things around. A festival is no place for this kind of acting out. There's kids running around and there'll be judges heading your way tomorrow or the next day. You're going to straighten up, right?"

Reuben's lip curled back in a snarl. "I'll do better than that. I'll clear out for a while. Give these jokers time to see what real work is like, since they think they're so smart." The snarl became even more pronounced. And before Lulu could blink, he'd stormed off.

Back in the Graces' tent, Pink became more relaxed. "Here I am, thinking I'm simply going to check in with my friends. Next thing I know, I'm having to break up a fight that one of those good friends is involved in. Let me have a nip of sweet tea if you don't mind." He listened for a second. "At least it's all quiet over there now."

Cherry snorted. "Only because that loudmouth isn't at the booth. Guess he'll get it all out of his system and come back. I don't think Reuben trusts his team to be able to cook worth a flip, and I'm sure he'll be back soon to supervise."

Flo walked into the booth, minus Coco and Ella Beth.

"Lulu, I spotted Derrick coming into the park and the girls wanted him to walk around with them for a few minutes. I hope that's okay."

"They probably aren't wanting to spend too much more time here today," said Lulu. "So a few minutes with Derrick before I take them home sounds like a good plan. And thanks so much, Flo, for walking the girls around."

Flo said, "Pink, is your presence here due to wanting to visit with the Graces or more of an official capacity? I wasn't sure what to think when I heard all that ruckus next door. That's why I hightailed it out of here with the girls."

Pink explained to a wide-eyed Flo what had happened.

"Y'all," Flo said, "that booth is officially trouble. I hope that's the end of the worst of it, though. Maybe now things will calm down a little."

Pink frowned at the Graces' wrists. "Are y'all planning on staying all night? I see you've got team wristbands on so you can stay after the gates are closed. Because I'm wondering if those folks next door might get riled up again later . . . after they have more to drink."

The Graces glanced at one another. Flo said, "I hate bringing this up, but my allergies are getting to me or something. My head is positively pounding and I need to get some sleep. Or I need somebody to run home for me and pick up my headache medicine and bring it to me, if I've got to stay."

Cherry said quickly, "I'm planning on staying to make sure the grill temperatures stay consistent. I can do that by myself. The only thing I wanted to do this afternoon was to visit one of my girlfriends real quick—she and her husband have a booth that's not too far away. But that won't take me long."

Evelyn hesitated. "I can stay here overnight if you need me to, Cherry. Not that I can cook, but I can lift and I could help you out if the people next door start creating any problems."

"No, that doesn't really make any sense," said Flo to Evelyn. "I knew going in that I was going to be here twenty-four hours a day with this barbeque. Don't worry about it, honey. A little headache won't take me down."

"How about," asked Lulu slowly as she figured it out, "if Flo leaves now with the girls? Ella Beth and Coco have got to be getting tired of walking. Flo could take them to Aunt Pat's or back to the house and then she can go home and sleep until right before they close the gates for the night. I can stay and help Cherry out—not officially, of course. I won't be cooking, but just making sure everything is okay. Then I'll leave when they close the gates and Flo can spend the night here with Cherry."

Flo glanced at her watch. "That would give me plenty of time to sleep or rest my eyes. I'll go ahead and help you round the girls up now, Lulu."

Lulu had to stop herself from giving seasoning tips or for actually helping Cherry cook. Instead, she stepped more into a hostess role like she had at the restaurant—visiting with the invited guests that came to the Graces' booth. Once Cherry had cooked up a bunch of barbeque, she hurried off to visit with her friend in the other booth while Lulu helped entertain the guests. And between the three Graces, they'd invited a ton of guests. There were folks in and out of there all the time—eating barbeque, drinking, and cutting up. Lulu herself ended up sampling quite a bit of barbeque. She ruefully patted her tummy. She could use an antacid.

At about eleven thirty, Flo hurried into the booth. "Lulu, thanks so much for spelling me—I feel like a million dollars now. You should probably be heading out of here—there's going to be thousands of folks leaving at one time and I'm sure you couldn't be parked close."

"It's okay, honey. It won't take me that long. Besides, you know I wore sensible shoes." She lifted up a foot encased in a tennis shoe. Maybe it didn't match her floral dress, but those shoes had served her well today. "And I've also brought my boots for the mud on the way to the car."

"Any more problems from the booth next door?" asked Flo.

"No, it's been pretty quiet over there," said Evelyn.

"Probably because Reuben stalked off to make a point," muttered Cherry.

"Funny that we didn't hear him come back," said

Lulu. "He seemed like he was dead set on bossing around the others and running that whole booth."

"Except," drawled Evelyn, "that he wanted to teach them a lesson. Maybe this is the lesson . . . showing them how tough life is without his expert advice."

It still seemed peculiar. But Lulu needed to get to her car before everyone else made an exodus for the parking. "All right . . . better go. I love y'all. Be careful."

Cherry hugged her. "Thanks for helping us hold down the fort, Lulu! You're the best."

The weather had actually not been bad for most of the day—a real blessing. However, it picked that very moment to pour down buckets. "Oh no!" gasped Flo. "Your pretty 'do, Lulu!"

"It'll be okay. I've got to wash it anyway," said Lulu with a laugh.

Cherry dug through a pile of things in the corner of the booth. "Where are our ponchos? Why do things disappear around here?"

"Don't worry about it, y'all. There's a bit of cardboard here and I'll hold it up over my head and kind of deflect it," said Lulu.

"Might could check your pocketbook and see if there's something you could cover yourself with in there, Lulu," said Evelyn with a chuckle. "That pocketbook of yours is big enough to use to backpack the Appalachian Trail."

Lulu laughed good-naturedly at her, but then snapped

her fingers and riffled through the bag real quick. Then she sighed. "I must have used that plastic rain bonnet another time and forgotten to replace it. No, there's nothing in my pocketbook that will do me a lick of good in this rain."

Flo said, "Don't we have an extra tarp or two, Cherry? That we didn't end up using for anything? We left them here, didn't we, just in case we needed them? Because cardboard is going to fall apart with this much rain."

Cherry made a gargling cry of frustration. "We did. And where are they?" Her eyes darkened. "I bet they're next door and that stupid Reuben swiped them."

"Now, Cherry!" said Flo. "Let's don't go picking a fight with that tent. You know how they are."

"I won't go accusing them, but let's poke around on the outskirts. I bet they took the tarps. Reuben even had a small covered storage area for food and supplies, remember? Like an annexed storage room. Let's stick our heads in there and see. They have my name on them, so it's not like we'll have to argue about who they belong to."

Cherry was determined, so Lulu offered to go with her. Flo and Evelyn didn't want anything to do with poking through the other booth's supplies. It was pitch-black dark and loud. There was music blaring from different booths and laughter and loud talking. The air was thick with the grilling smoke and cast a murky fog over the festival. First Cherry and Lulu poked around the nooks and crannies between their booth and the next. Then Cherry pointed a finger to a small tent that annexed onto a back "room" of the bigger booth. It was about the size of a standard closet.

Lulu at this point was ready to get out of the rain. She and Cherry stuck their heads into the storage tent. Lulu felt her heart start pounding hard in her chest and she put a hand up as if to stop it. With her other hand she grabbed Cherry and they backed out and into the rain as fast as they'd gotten out of it.

Because Reuben Shaw was lying dead, with a butcher knife stuck in his chest. And covered by the Graces' tarp, marked with Cherry's name in permanent marker.

Chapter

4

They were lucky that Pink was still at the festival and was one of the policemen who responded to their call. He had a very calming effect on the women, who were left pale and shaking from the emotional experience of finding a body—even the body of someone who hadn't been very pleasant. The fact was that he'd been alive and talking to them only hours before, then had reached a horrible end. He'd had his life unnaturally shortened and no one deserved that.

Pink stayed right there with them in their booth while the Memphis police questioned them. The booth next door was marked off with crime scene tape and the police created a barrier to keep people from getting too close and tampering with the scene. Eventually, an ambulance arrived to remove the body. A Lieutenant Avery Clark interviewed the women and even asked Pink a couple of questions after learning that he'd witnessed the argument earlier.

Cherry was ready to ask some questions of her own. "Shouldn't y'all be talking to his team members? They're the ones who were either threatening to kill Reuben or were putting him in a choke hold."

Lieutenant Clark regarded her steadily. "We surely will. But right now we're focusing on the people who discovered the body, whose tarp was found covering the body, and who actually assaulted the victim earlier in the day."

Cherry turned as red as her hair. "Well, all right then. But it wasn't really like that." Her voice was uncharacteristically hesitant.

"What *was* it like then?" asked the policeman, giving her a stern look over his glasses. He was an older cop who didn't seem in the mood to have his time wasted.

Lulu cleared her throat. "I think Cherry means that she was trying to protect Reuben's teammate, Sharon, from him. He was acting very threateningly and Cherry used a nondeadly weapon to prevent him from hurting her."

"The teammate," said Lieutenant Clark, raising an eyebrow, "who was threatening to kill him?"

"So she's not exactly a pushover. Still, he was a lot bigger than she was and he meant business. Hitting him over the head with a plaster Elvis wasn't the wrong thing to do. I'd do it again, as a matter of fact. Except I'd choose something besides Elvis as a weapon. I feel like I was desecrating the King," said Cherry.

"And remind me again what you two were doing in the storage tent of the booth next door?" asked the policeman smoothly. The lines around Pink's eyes crinkled in concern, as if the women needed to be sure to think through their answer.

Lulu said, "I was fixing to leave the festival before the gates closed." She pointed to her wristband-free wrist. "Of course, it was pouring down rain, same as it is now. Umbrellas aren't allowed at the festival, you know, so we were searching for tarps. We thought if I held a tarp over my head that I might stay dryer on my way to the car."

Cherry added darkly, "And swiping our stuff would be typical of the immature kind of thing I'd expect Reuben to do. So after we poked around here looking for it, I mentioned that maybe we should take a peek in his booth's storage area."

Both women were quiet for a moment, thinking about what they'd seen there. Somebody hadn't been crazy about Reuben. And they'd shown their displeasure with a butcher knife.

"What was your opinion of the other team members?" asked Lieutenant Clark. "Did you get along okay? What was the problem between them and Reuben?"

Cherry shrugged. "They weren't the most fun-loving

people to be around, but I guess that's because they acted really stressed out. But they were better than Reuben. They're probably fine under ordinary circumstances, but were worse when they were around Reuben."

Lulu said, "And of course lately they'd been around Reuben for twenty-four hours a day. From what I could tell about Reuben, he was especially hard to deal with when he was being competitive."

"He was one of those people who thought he knew best all the time. Plus, he wanted to win. So he was being a real jerk, from what I could see," said Cherry with fire in her eyes.

"What about the other man, Brody?" asked Pink. "How did he figure in? I know he was Sharon's husband, but what was his connection with Reuben?"

Cherry said, "I think he was a friend of Reuben's. Although they sure weren't friendly yesterday."

Lieutenant Clark closed his worn leather notebook. "Okay, that's going to be it for now. I'm going to want to talk to you later, Cherry, so make sure you're not planning on leaving Memphis."

Cherry snorted. "Leaving Memphis? I'll be lucky if I even leave this booth. We've had Evelyn in charge of the food for the last couple of hours, so who knows what kind of catching up I'm going to have to do. Or what perfectly good food I'll have to throw into the garbage. It's okay if I stay here, isn't it?" she asked suddenly, frowning. "I mean, with the crime scene next door."

"It's okay as long as you stay in this booth and don't visit that one," said the policeman in a clipped voice as he walked out of their booth.

"Don't worry about catching up with the cooking. Flo was helping, too," reminded Lulu. "Everything will be just fine."

When Lulu's alarm went off the next morning, she was genuinely surprised and felt certain she had a few more hours of sleep. Of course, it had been a really short night, after the police interview and everything. Then Pink had escorted her out to the parking lot so she could finally get home and rest.

She'd wanted to check in at Aunt Pat's and make sure everything was going well before she made it over to the Graces' booth.

Aunt Pat's was quiet when Lulu arrived at eight in the morning, and wouldn't start bustling until the diners started coming in at eleven. As usual, she felt a real sense of peace as soon as she walked into the dining room and saw the familiar wooden booths, red-checkered table-cloths, and creaky hardwood floors. You couldn't even see the restaurant walls because they were covered with photographs and memorabilia of all types and descriptions. As usual, the framed black-and-white photo of Lulu's gently smiling Aunt Pat helped her relax. It looked like she was about to hop off the wall and visit with her.

The kitchen wasn't quite as still as the dining room had been. There Ben was busily checking off a food delivery and putting it away. It was a large one, too . . . always a good sign in this business. They must have really gone through some food at the restaurant recently.

Sara was also checking things off the order sheet and putting them away. "Can I help?" asked Lulu. They both waved her off and kept counting.

The tables were even already set up for the day, with fresh paper towel rolls on each table and clean checkered tablecloths and silverware all set to go. The old wooden floor shone. Either they'd worked their tails off after the restaurant closed last night, or they had brought in so much temporary help that it only took minutes to get it in tip-top shape.

Seeing nothing to do, and feeling a bit befuddled about it, Lulu retreated to the sanctuary of the front porch. She was delighted to see her friend Morty already there. Morty was one-third of the Back Porch Blues Band, a regular customer of Aunt Pat's for the past sixty years, and a good friend. He was in his eighties and resembled a black version of Mr. Clean. Although he kept calling himself retired, you couldn't tell it. He and his friends Big Ben and Buddy still played regular gigs at Aunt Pat's, and any wedding or even funeral that they could be booked for.

"What's going on, Lulu? You were frowning up a

storm when you came out on the porch. Everything going okay in the kitchen?"

"The kitchen is great—no problems there. But wait until you hear what happened to Cherry and me last night," said Lulu and launched into the story. It was good to sort out some of the details by telling them to her friend.

"Do you think that Cherry will get into any trouble?" asked Morty, eyebrows drawing together. "Considering the argument she had, and the fact that it was even witnessed by a police officer . . . and then y'all discovering the body—that's sort of suspicious, isn't it?"

"I sure hope she won't get into any trouble," said Lulu. "They've got to realize that Cherry wouldn't have been in any hurry to search in that storage tent if she'd thought there was a body in it. Especially a body wrapped in a tarp with her name on it."

Morty said, "Who was on pig duty at the barbeque pit?"

"Cherry was. And I was right there with her the whole time while Evelyn was hostess to the different guests who came in the booth."

"I'd say that's an alibi and a half if she had y'all there to vouch that she was cooking spare ribs all night," said Morty.

Lulu shifted in her rocker, suddenly feeling uncomfortable. "Morty, there's a problem there. Flo left yesterday afternoon with a headache and I took her spot until midnight. Cherry did leave the booth for a short while last night. She has this good friend of hers with a booth and she left to visit a spell with her."

"Well, that's all right then. So that woman will give her the alibi and everything will work out fine," said Morty.

Lulu shook her head. "It's not that easy, I'm afraid. Cherry had a hard time finding her friend's booth. It was dark, you know, and foggy. And loud. While she was looking, there were some folks who came up to talk to her—you know, because she was dressed like Elvis."

"Did those people have names and could give her an alibi?" asked Morty.

"She had no idea who they were, so no. Basically, it boils down to the fact that if Cherry had really wanted to kill Reuben, she had the opportunity to do it. And I guess there were enough butcher knives at that festival that she also had the means to do it—along with thousands of other people. Of course, none of us believe that Cherry would murder anybody."

Morty said, "You've got me all worried now. I'd sure hate anything to happen to Cherry. Maybe I can get friendly with the other team and find out some information for you, too."

"That sounds like a good plan, Morty. You could maybe even offer to help Sharon and Brody out for a while, since Reuben isn't there cooking with them anymore.

Besides, folks always like talking with you." Lulu reached over and gave her friend a hug. "And I do, too."

Cherry was definitely in a funk at the grill. "Nothing is going right. I'm so distracted that I hardly even recollect what spices I've used on the ribs. The tent next door has gone from being too loud with arguments to being too quiet. And the police keep popping their heads in to talk to me like they think I have something to do with all this. That Lieutenant What's-his-face."

Evelyn drawled, "Well, clearly the police haven't found anything that would pin this murder on you or you wouldn't be at the festival—you'd be cooling your heels in jail."

Cherry glared at Evelyn as she shook out what appeared to Lulu like a heap of cayenne onto her barbeque. "Somehow the thought of being in jail isn't cheering me up too much, Evelyn."

Morty was looking askance at the cayenne, too. "You don't have to worry about going to jail, Cherry—you didn't do anything. And since you're innocent, they won't discover any evidence that could make them take you in."

Cherry was still put out. "Except for a tarp with my name on it that wrapped up the body like a present. What a dumb night for me to wander around the festival. If I'd only stayed in the booth, they wouldn't even be considering me as a suspect. I wasn't planning on being gone for very long—I was just poking my head out for a few minutes after spending all day with that barbeque."

"I'm wondering what's going on with Sharon and Brody next door," said Lulu in a low voice. "Are they shocked at what happened? Do you think one of them did it?"

Evelyn raised an eyebrow. "Well, of course one of them did it. Neither of them could stand Reuben. We know Cherry didn't do it. And it sure doesn't seem to be some random act of violence at the festival."

"Somebody's got to be pretty mad to stick a butcher knife into a man," said Morty.

"But this was the kind of man who probably made tons of people mad at him. He made Cherry mad at him and she barely even knew him," said Lulu.

Morty stood up. "I'm going to head next door and see if I can sweet-talk my way into their booth and sample their barbeque. Just to get an idea of what the mood over there is like and what kind of information they might have."

Lulu nodded. "It would be good to get your impression of them. I'll head over there soon. I brought goodies from the restaurant and I'll offer them to the Jensons as sort of a sympathy gift."

Morty left for the next tent and Lulu noticed that someone was standing at the edge of the Graces' booth. "Is someone officially on hostess duty?" she murmured. "We've got a guest."

Cherry was still cooking and Evelyn was in no hurry to move, so Flo hurried over. "Can we help you? Oh," she said, peering closer at their guest, who was looking meek and taking off a baseball cap to uncover dark hair with a white skunk-like stripe down the middle. "It's . . . John, isn't it?"

"The John Smith who so conveniently disappeared into thin air as soon as we got into trouble?" growled Cherry, turning around and brandishing her metal spatula. "Pardon me if I don't jump up and down with joy."

John seemed chastened.

"That's the reason I came by," he said, looking them each in the eye with difficulty. "I wanted to apologize for my ungentlemanly behavior yesterday. When tensions escalated in that tent, I should have stepped in and defused them. Instead, I took off. Y'all must really think poorly of me."

Actually, Lulu had plumb forgotten about the man, in the wake of all the commotion. But it was kind of odd that he'd seemed almost afraid of the argument that was going on in the booth.

"My parents always argued a lot when I was a kid, and my whole adult life I've tried to avoid any kind of conflict at all. It grates on my nerves so bad that I can't stand to be around it. But y'all deserved better than that . . . I'm sorry." John's gray eyes were solemn and embarrassed, too.

Flo quickly said, "Hon, I know how that can be. Don't

think a thing about it." But Flo didn't like conflict, either, and she hadn't even witnessed the scene yesterday because she was taking the girls around the festival.

Cherry, who'd been staring studiously at the grill while John had been talking, turned and looked sideways at him. "It's okay, John. Sounds like life wasn't much fun for you growing up. I can see how you wouldn't want to see stuff like that as a grown-up, either."

"Are we friends again?" he asked anxiously.

"Friends!" they chimed in.

"Why don't you sit down with us for a few minutes and sample our barbeque," said Evelyn.

He glanced at his watch. "That sounds good to me. I've got a few minutes."

Flo said, "You got to meet up with your ride to go home?"

"Oh no. No, I've got a booth here myself," said John. "But I'm part of a big team and we're rotating in and out, so I'm taking a break now. With a small team like this, though, you'd have to be here almost all the time."

"Or we *should* be here all the time," said Cherry darkly, still thinking about her little alibi problem.

John sat down at a table and they served him up some ribs. He took a bite and his eyebrows rose in surprise. "Hey, this is good stuff!"

The women laughed. Flo said, "Well, of course it is, honey! Did you think we couldn't cook?"

"If they can't cook, then I've made a really terrible investment of my money," said Evelyn drily.

John took another bite of the pork and chewed for a minute before answering. "I guess I saw the campy Elvis stuff and thought y'all were here to have a good time and couldn't really cook. My stomach is glad to find out that I was wrong."

"We're here to have a good time, but part of our good time always revolves around food," said Cherry.

John shifted uncomfortably. "With the situation going on at the booth next door, I'm thinking it hasn't been fun all the time. Did it ever settle down over there?"

Cherry snorted. Lulu said, "Define 'settle down.'" At John's confused expression, Lulu said, "The arguing stopped over there. But the fellow who was causing all the trouble is still managing to make some from beyond the grave—he's been murdered."

"What?" John's eyes opened up wide. He sure didn't like conflict; that was a fact. Even so, it seemed like a big reaction from someone who didn't even know the man.

Lulu said, "It was last night. Reuben Shaw, who was the one everyone was mad at yesterday afternoon, was stabbed and stuck in a storage area at the booth next door."

"Lulu and I discovered the body," said Cherry with disbelief in her voice as if she was having a hard time coming to grips with it all.

John said seriously, "Do the police know what happened? Did they catch who did it?"

Lulu shook her head. "They sure don't know, but they're talking to everyone to try to find out. They talked to Cherry and me a long time since we witnessed the argument next door and also discovered the body."

"The tension in that booth was running high yesterday," said John, shifting uncomfortably just thinking about it. "I could tell, even for the short time I was over there, that they were all furious with each other."

Lulu said, "There was a lot of anger there. Clearly, since they started fighting with each other. But some of it might have been people who were spending too much time together and were getting on each other's nerves."

"I guess that's only natural," said John. "Well, I wanted to let y'all know that I was sorry. You're nice to feed me, especially under the circumstances." He stared down at his empty plate.

"Don't spend another minute worrying about it," said Lulu.

"Guess I'd better get back to my booth now," John said with a sheepish smile. "Otherwise, I'll be on their bad side, too."

He stood up to leave and narrowly missed running into Sharon on his way out. He muttered a quick apology as he hurried out of the booth.

Sharon peered after him for a second, then turned back to the women. Her eyes were red and her face blotchy as if she'd been crying. She soon started crying again as she said, "Y'all. I am just so sorry. You must think I'm awful!" She'd put on a lot of eye makeup, probably to distract from the exhausted circles under her eyes. Her crying made her mascara trickle down her face in rivers.

It was clearly the day for apologies. The women hurried over to soothe Sharon and find her some barbeque . . . and a few tissues. At this rate, there wouldn't be any barbeque left for the judges to sample. Still, in times of trouble, food always hit the spot and made everything better, at least temporarily. Sharon sat down at the red-and-white checkerboard-covered table and ate ribs with such abandon that the other women couldn't help joining in. Although after this festival, Lulu was sure she wouldn't be eating much barbeque for a while. Or maybe not too much of anything, considering the couple of extra pounds she'd put on. It was about time for a diet. Which was hard to do when you owned a barbeque restaurant.

Lulu said, "We don't think you're awful at all, Sharon."

"We could tell there was a lot of tension over there in that booth. You saw how mad Reuben made me, and I only spent a few minutes with him," said Cherry, growing flushed as she remembered. "I know we're not supposed to speak ill of the dead, but that guy was a handful. I don't blame y'all at all for squabbling with him."

Flo said, "I did have a question for you, though, hon. Something has been bothering me about the whole thing. Why on earth would you share a booth with the man when he was such a troll? I'd have thought you and Brody would've steered clear of him, and here you are signing up to spend three days straight or more with him."

"In a confined space, too," said Lulu.

Cherry shuddered at the notion.

"I guess that does seem pretty confusing," said Sharon with a sigh, rubbing her eyes in exhaustion. "But he didn't used to be such a rascal. Reuben was always a lot of fun. Sometimes he'd have these crazy kinds of ideas for stuff to do, but we always ended up having a good time. One time he convinced Brody to go hang gliding with him. Another time, he and Brody went skydiving. Reuben could be real convincing, too, when he wanted to be. The only thing he couldn't get Brody to do was bungee jumping, and that's because Brody always gets cricks in his neck as it is."

"So he was real persuasive about getting a Rock and Ribs booth, too?" asked Evelyn. "I wouldn't have said he was a charmer. I'm pretty sure that I could have resisted him."

Sharon said, "You probably could have, but maybe not so much when he was at the top of his game. He could charm the birds right out of the trees." She smiled wistfully, remembering. "And yes, he did want to have a booth real bad. He was always bragging about his barbeque, saying it was the best stuff you ever put in your mouth. He came to the festival every year and charmed his way into all the booths to sample the barbeque. He got to be everybody's best friend, and to him, it was one big party."

"Was he always the way he was the last few days?" asked Lulu. "Seems like y'all would be worried about sharing a booth with him if that were the case."

Sharon shook her head. "No, he sure wasn't. He was a great guy with a huge personality who loved doing fun things—really, he was like a big kid. But then something happened about two years ago and he suddenly changed . . . almost overnight. All of a sudden he wasn't this carefree kind of guy anymore."

Lulu frowned. "That does sound real sudden. And you don't know what made him change?"

Cherry snapped her fingers. "I got it—he probably went through a divorce, right? Divorce can really mess somebody up."

"He was divorced, yes. But he got divorced from his wife right after this all started, so I know that doesn't have anything to do with it," said Sharon.

"Hmm. That's a mystery, all right," said Cherry.

"So how did you end up together doing the festival?" asked Lulu.

"Reuben called us out of the blue," said Sharon. "He was suddenly real enthusiastic about Rock and Ribs and having a booth there. He was almost like the old

Reuben—excited, happy, full of life. He asked us to join him on his team. He sounded certain we could win it."

"And you decided to let bygones be bygones?" asked Evelyn, lifting her eyebrows.

"That's right," said Sharon. "We were so glad to hear the old Reuben that we decided we'd go along with his idea. So Brody asked off from work and we all got set to cook barbeque. Of course, we had no idea it was going to end up like this. Reuben was in an awful mood right off the bat. He was drinking a lot, too, and Reuben had never been a great drinker. Soon he was talking in a real abusive way and even made a pass at me a couple of times—which was why Brody was so furious with him and felt like he had to defend my honor."

"He had every right to be furious with him," said Cherry, looking furious herself.

Flo shook her head, "Alcohol really can change a person. Reckon that's what the whole change in personality thing was from?"

Sharon shrugged. "I don't know. Maybe. All I know is he was different in every way. He even started having problems with work stuff. I kept hearing on the grapevine that people were real unhappy with him as a contractor. That guy, who was just in here? He was one of them."

The women stared at Sharon. "John?" asked Lulu. "You mean the fellow who almost ran into you when you were coming in the booth? You know him?"

"I don't know him at all. But Reuben did. He talked about it when he wasn't busy yelling at us all. The guy was unhappy with some contract work Reuben did at his house. Real unhappy. He wouldn't pay him and said Reuben was using shoddy materials and poor workmanship. They've been fighting on and off about the job for months apparently. Reuben said the guy even came over to his house sometimes, yelling about the work and demanding that Reuben come over to fix it."

Lulu and Cherry exchanged glances. This was something they wanted to talk over, but would rather not do it with Sharon right in front of them. Instead, Lulu quickly changed the subject. "Mmm. It's a small world, isn't it? By the way, Sharon, how are you going to finish out the competition? Aren't you shorthanded now?"

Sharon sighed. "Yes. We might need help. We want to finish what we started, but Reuben was primarily the cook. Brody and I are handling it okay, but we could use a couple of extra hands, for sure."

Life has a way of handing good things out sometimes. Morty, who'd been hanging out with Brody, walked back into the Graces' booth. He cleared his throat. "As it happens, I've got a clear schedule for the next twenty-four hours. And when I can't be here, I know my friend Buddy or Big Ben can sub for me. Or maybe we can all work a shift together. I might be old," he said, drawing himself up with dignity, "but I can sure cook."

"Amen to that," said Lulu. "Y'all would be lucky to have them on your team, Sharon."

"I'm not one for turning down unexpected blessings," said Sharon, holding out her hand to shake Morty's. "Welcome to our team!"

Chapter 5

"Interesting how John never mentioned that he knew Reuben, even after we were talking about the booth next door," said Lulu shortly after Sharon returned to her booth.

"Or even when he heard that Reuben had been murdered," said Cherry, agreeing.

"We should talk to John," said Lulu. "But we'll need to figure out which booth is his."

Cherry crowed and rubbed her hands together. "Lulu is on the case! Woo-hoo!"

Lulu said mildly, "I don't have any choice, do I? One of my best friends is a suspect and I need to clear her name."

Cherry beamed at her. "Indeed you do. And I'm more

than ready for my name to be cleared. Although I don't think Pink considers me the strongest suspect."

"I don't know," drawled Evelyn from behind them. "You sure did attack the man, from all the accounts I've heard. With an Elvis. Redheads and tempers are well known."

Cherry gave her a cross look. "Yeah, I might have killed him in the heat of the moment. I sure wouldn't have thought about it, chilled out, then planned to sneak over there later and stab the guy. Not my style," she said with a sniff.

Evelyn laughed. "Well, I'm glad to hear that, considering I'm spending all this time in an enclosed space with you. Premeditated crime is a lot worse than heat of the moment."

But with the same end result, thought Lulu. "So how are we going to find this booth?" said Lulu. "Did y'all ever see what direction John was heading in when he left here?"

"No, he's a slippery rascal," said Flo. "He was always popping in and out real sudden."

"Maybe he apparates," suggested Evelyn, languidly taking a sip of her wine.

Cherry said, "Guess we'll be getting our exercise. There's about a mile's worth of booths here."

"Did anybody catch his last name?" asked Lulu.

"Did he throw it?" asked Cherry.

"Remember? He said his name was John Smith," said

Flo with certainty. "And I've got to wonder if his last name is Smith."

"You think he gave us a phony name?" asked Lulu.

Flo said consideringly, "I don't know. He was obviously hiding stuff from us so maybe that was why I got the impression that there was something phony about him."

"Who's cooking for us?" asked Evelyn, alarmed. "You and Lulu are both going? Don't we have a judge or somebody coming by? I haven't even put my eyelashes on."

Flo said, "Don't worry about it, Evelyn. I'll cook, and you can serve it up if we have visitors come by. Besides, we've pretty much cooked all the ribs . . . we've got to figure out the best to send into the judging tent for judging."

"With all the excitement, I'd almost forgotten that y'all were in a competition." said Lulu. "Have you heard back from the judges at all?"

"Well, we didn't win for best decorated booth, but that's no surprise," said Cherry. "Did you happen to see some of those booths? They're like mansions. The one that won was two stories tall, with a party deck on the top with umbrellas and covered with Slovak flags. We were still messing around with tarps."

"We were in the Patio Porkers competition, Cherry. The cooking area is only fifteen square feet," drawled Evelyn. "We couldn't exactly make a mansion with those specs."

Cherry was still grumbling. "At least we had flooring, but that was as elaborate as we got. Maybe we'll do better with the spare ribs contest." But she didn't sound convinced.

There were tons of booths. Lulu and Cherry first started peering into them and searching for John. But then Lulu realized that they might even go to the right booth and John could be temporarily out—visiting another booth or even at the restroom. So they returned to the booths and asked whether they had a John on their team.

Of course, many people did have a John on their team. Cherry and Lulu then had to think up a quick description of their John. The skunk-like stripe on the top of his head did help.

They'd gone to twenty booths before finally someone recognized their description. "Yeah, I know which guy you're talking about. He's over in that booth down there," he said, pointing. "He's on the same team as a buddy of mine."

It was the right booth. But John wasn't there.

"You couldn't find him?" asked Evelyn. "Did his team at least know how to find him apart from the festival? Where does this guy live?"

Lulu said, "That's where we ended up making progress. We got a home address for John. So now we don't have to worry about chasing him down at the festival."

"And thank goodness for that," said Cherry. "I couldn't stand to do any more walking around searching for him. My feet are killing me!"

"Maybe if you'd ditch the men's shoes," said Flo with a snort. "Imitating Elvis can only be taken so far."

"The whole thing is wretchedly disappointing," said Evelyn with a plaintive note in her voice. "I thought he was trying to have a romance with Flo or Lulu or me. The single ladies, you know."

Flo said slyly, "I think it was Lulu who was the source of the attraction."

Lulu gave a hooting laugh. "Mercy! No! Absolutely not. Even if he was interested, there's no way I'd train another man. I'm too old. Not after all these years."

The Graces laughed. But more than likely, they agreed with her.

"Besides," said Lulu, "I know why John was hanging out with the Graces."

"It wasn't because of our charm and beauty?" asked Evelyn.

"I'm afraid not. I think he wanted to keep an eye on Reuben. If he'd been harassing Reuben, like Sharon was saying, then maybe he was looking for a good time to make trouble here at the festival."

Cherry said, "That weasel! Telling us he doesn't like conflict. Skipping out on us because he was so *sensitive*. A bunch of hooey!"

"Wait. I'm confused," said Flo, squinting her eyes and studying Lulu. "So are you saying that John hung out in our booth to sort of scope out the area? Then he found a chance to take Reuben out with a butcher knife? Doesn't that seem kind of extreme?"

"Not to mention risky," said Evelyn. "What if Reuben had seen him?"

"I'm wondering if maybe he did see him," said Lulu. "Remember in the excitement of the fight? I thought that Reuben seemed to recognize someone or seemed like he was going to say something before he stopped. Maybe he'd spotted John before John slipped away."

"Like I was saying," said Evelyn, "risky."

Cherry said, "You know, maybe he wasn't really planning on murdering Reuben. Maybe he simply wanted to get back at him on a real simple level."

"You're right, Cherry," said Lulu. "What if John planned some other kind of mischief for revenge? Maybe he was planning on ruining his barbeque by pouring something into the cooked meat. There's lots of things he could have done on a much smaller scale."

"Or maybe," said Evelyn, "he *did* kill Reuben. Because he sure has done a disappearing act now."

Lulu said, "But isn't it funny that he came by to see us after the murder? He acted like he didn't know what had happened."

"Because he was pumping us for information," said Evelyn. "Remember how curious he was about what the police were saying and how we'd found the body and all? He was on a reconnaissance mission so he could protect himself better from being discovered."

"Yeah, and smooth things over with us so we weren't still mad at him. Mad people might start putting two and two together and wondering why he cut out of there while that fight was going on," said Flo.

"I say he's dirty," said Cherry, viciously poking at the barbeque. "And Lulu, let's plan on showing up at his house real soon. I want to surprise him, all right."

"Maybe surprise him enough to shoot y'all in his foyer," drawled Evelyn.

Lulu said, "I was thinking more that we would go to his house and park in front of his neighbor's house and wait for him to come outside. I'd rather talk to John in full view of the outside world. Just in case."

Derrick came by the booth with the twins.

Lulu gave them all a hug. "Girls," she said, "how about if I take y'all around the festival for a while? I haven't had a chance to really see what all is out there."

Coco said, "Can we see the singing contest?"

"There are judges and only the best singers keep from getting booted off," said Ella Beth. "And the audience gets to help choose!"

"Sure thing. It sounds like a lot of fun. Maybe we can buy some slushies to drink while we watch—it feels like it's starting to really heat up," said Lulu.

Evelyn said, "By the way, Derrick, you know I've been operating as official hostess here at the Graces' booth. We've had a heap of people . . . personal guests, of course . . . come through here and they've raved over the tee shirts. I've heard so many nice things said about them."

"Me, too!" said Flo. "Everybody has said how clever they are and how much they love them."

"And thank heavens for them," said Evelyn. "I couldn't have abided staying dressed up as Ms. Priscilla Presley the whole time. That getup was way too hot to wear for very long."

Derrick's face lit up with the praise. It was amazing, thought Lulu, how long the process of restoring a child's self-esteem took. His mother had really done a number on him before Sara and Ben took Derrick in to live with them and the twins.

"That's great," he said with relief. "I felt kind of bad that we didn't win the tee shirt contest."

"Pooh on those judges," said Cherry stoutly, waving around her spatula in a threatening manner. "They wouldn't know a winning tee shirt if it came up and bit them on the behind. I've heard tons of compliments, too, Derrick. Thanks so much for doing that design for us." She gave him a one-armed but enthusiastic hug.

Derrick looked like he might float, he was flying so high from the praise. If people looked past the tattoos and the piercings and the tough exterior, they'd find a really sweet and insecure boy.

"Well," Derrick said gruffly, "I guess I'd better head on out. I'm meeting Peaches here in a few minutes. And after we hang out here for a while, I've got some other stuff I need to do."

The Graces beamed at him. Peaches was absent Grace Peggy Sue's step-granddaughter and they doted on her. "Isn't that *nice* that you and Peaches are going to hang out together," said Flo. "Oh, I am so glad to hear that y'all are still dating each other."

Lulu found her pocketbook and opened her fat wallet to find a little money, which she shoved in Derrick's hand. "Here. Buy her some food and a drink. And have fun, sweetie."

The festival was absolutely jam-packed with people. The fact that it was the weekend combined with a rare period of sunshine meant that the crowds had arrived in droves. Ella Beth and Coco had come to the festival hungry, so Lulu was soon digging in her purse again for money. They ended up eating funnel cakes, washed down with slushies.

"Mercy," said Lulu, "I think we need to go home and brush our teeth now, girls."

"Oh, Granny Lulu. We'll be fine. It wasn't all that much sugar," said Coco.

The entire snack had been constructed of sugar.

"Look! The show's starting!" said Ella Beth.

It was a transfixing show, and the girls and Lulu happily spent more time than Lulu even realized had passed, watching the different contestants try to claim the prize.

She glanced at her watch. "Girls, it's time for us to head back to the booth. Y'all are pretty pink and I am, too. Do you have sunscreen on?" Of course they didn't. Ben and Sara were scrambling too much at the restaurant, and teenage boys didn't think about stuff like sunscreen. Nor did nine-year-old girls.

"Guess what, Granny Lulu?" asked Coco, carefully skirting a tremendous mud puddle. "I can Hula-hoop one hundred and fifty times!"

"Mercy!" said Lulu again. Unfortunately, she'd somehow managed to step right in the tremendous mud puddle. There was now a squelching noise coming from her sensible sandals.

Ella Beth said, "That's only because it wasn't a real Hula-hoop. It was on the Wii, so it doesn't count."

Lulu wasn't one hundred percent sure that she knew what a Wii was.

"Does, too! You're jealous because you couldn't make it go around that many times," said Coco.

Ella Beth didn't appear to have an answer for this. Instead, she abruptly changed the subject.

"Did you know we saw one of our waiters at the festival yesterday?"

"Did you, sweetie? I'm amazed he was able to get away with the restaurant being so crazy," said Lulu.

Ella Beth said, "It was that waiter, Tim. You remember him. Pale and skinny? Sort of sad all the time?"

Ella Beth had fond hopes of becoming a detective

when she was older. "Yes, I think I know who you're talking about."

Coco said, "Yeah, but when you ran up to hug him, you didn't notice he was having an argument with that guy from the booth next to the Graces. Awk-*ward*!"

Lulu said quickly, "Coco . . . which man do you mean?"

"The loud one, the one that Auntie Flo had to drag us away from yesterday so we wouldn't hear him," said Coco.

"And Ella Beth, you gave this man a hug?"

"No, no, no. I was fixing to give Tim the waiter a hug. He plays Crazy Eights with me at Aunt Pat's sometimes. But Derrick stopped me because Tim was having an argument with that really loud guy." Ella Beth seemed disappointed that she hadn't been observant enough to see they'd been arguing.

"You didn't hear what they were arguing about?" asked Lulu.

"No. Because Coco started fussing with me about whose turn it was to sit in the front seat on the way back home," said Ella Beth.

Fortunately, before this argument was reincarnated, they were within sight of the Graces' booth and the girls raced each other to see who could get there first. They flew right past Derrick, who was approaching with his girlfriend, Peaches. It looked to be the perfect opportunity for her to talk to him without the twins being around.

At first glance, Peaches didn't seem like a natural match for Derrick. The girl was lovely with long blond hair, sparkling blue eyes, and the cutest clothes. She provided quite a contrast with Derrick and his dark clothes, piercings, and tattoos. Somehow, though, the balance worked.

Peaches gave Lulu a big hug. Lulu said, "Have y'all had a good time at the festival?"

"We sure have," said Peaches. "Derrick was sweet to buy me some food. I'm stuffed!" Her rosy cheeks dimpled in a smile.

Derrick grinned and said, "It wasn't exactly food technically."

"Half food, half drink? A fried Coca-Cola," said Peaches, grinning back at him.

"What?" asked Lulu, making a face.

"A fried Coke. They said it was really just Coke-flavored batter with more Coke, whipped cream, and cinnamon on top. You wouldn't believe how good it was," said Peaches.

She had that right.

"Well, sugar, I'm tickled that you enjoyed it. And you go home and really scrub those pretty teeth of yours." said Lulu. "Your grandmama will have our hides if we conspired to get you cavities. So y'all are still making the rounds here, right? Lots to do, lots to see. And no rain right now, so that's a good thing."

"Don't jinx us, Granny Lulu," Derrick said, peering apprehensively at the big clouds overhead.

"Before y'all go on your way, I was wondering if I could ask you something about yesterday, Derrick. Now, don't get all concerned on me"—Derrick's face had quickly clouded up as if thinking he'd done something wrong—"it's something the girls mentioned to me about our waiter."

"Oh," said Derrick, nodding, "that guy with the real dark hair. He's got to be dyeing it. What's his name . . . Tim."

"That's right. The girls say that y'all saw him yesterday," said Lulu.

"We did. Ella Beth was going to run up and give him a hug because they play cards together on the porch at the restaurant or something. But I stopped her because he and another guy were arguing about something," said Derrick.

"Thanks for putting the brakes on her. Did you hear what the men were arguing about?" asked Lulu.

"Not a whole lot. Actually, I was trying to listen in because they were so focused on each other and the other guy was so mad that they didn't even notice us—didn't even see a little girl running at them. I thought that was weird. The other guy, not Tim, was saying that Tim wasn't returning his messages or coming to his door."

Lulu said, "This guy that Tim was talking to, what did he look like?"

Derrick described a short, bald man. Reuben.

"What did Tim say when Reuben . . . that's the other guy, Derrick . . . complained about him not returning his messages?"

"Tim said he'd moved. And that he'd been busy. But then he said that he was tired of 'living his life like this.' Then that other guy, Reuben I guess, pulled him off by the arm to talk somewhere else." Derrick shrugged. "That's all I heard."

Lulu gave him a quick hug. "That's very, very helpful, Derrick. You were very observant to have seen and heard all that."

Peaches' blue eyes grew wide. "Are you investigating another case? Gran always talks about you being a gifted detective."

Lulu clucked. "Well, I wouldn't say that. I wouldn't say I was investigating or anything. I'm just poking around, checking things out."

"Is that because Cherry is in trouble?" asked Derrick, concerned. "I don't think she's really a serious suspect, but she did have an argument with that Reuben," said Lulu.

"Sounds like he was arguing with absolutely everybody," said Peaches. "Maybe it's not such a bad thing that he's not around anymore."

Chapter 6

Derrick and Peaches were off to explore more of the festival, and Evelyn offered to drive the twins back to the restaurant since she was leaving. Lulu decided she'd stay put at the booth and visit for a while. Morty, Buddy, and Big Ben arrived at the Graces' booth, so there was suddenly a lot of activity . . . and hugging. Morty and his friends comprised the Back Porch Blues Band, and now in their eighties, they'd had a relationship with both Lulu and Aunt Pat for decades. They were loyal regulars at the restaurant and played on the screen porch there quite a bit, too.

"I hear there's some cooking to be done," said Buddy. "Maybe there might be some eating, too?"

"What I can't figure out," said Big Ben, "is why the best cook at the whole festival isn't cooking."

"Shoot," said Morty, "you know that wouldn't be fair, Big Ben. If Lulu were to start cooking up Aunt Pat–style barbeque, the other guys wouldn't even have a shot at winning. It all has to be fair, you know. Besides, the rules say that professional cooks can't compete."

"I hear there's trouble afoot, too," said Big Ben in what he apparently thought was a whisper. "I know if Lulu is on it, then the case will be sewn up in no time."

"I bet Pink is kicking back and relaxing, knowing that Lulu is on the case," agreed Buddy.

Lulu sighed. "Y'all are sweet, but I have a feeling Pink is probably hoping I don't get involved. You know how trouble always springs up when I do."

"Sure enough," said Buddy, "but the mysteries end up getting solved, don't they?"

She couldn't really argue with that.

"So we'll mosey on next door and I'll introduce Big Ben and Buddy to Sharon and Brody," said Morty. "And if we happen to hear anything that might be a clue, we'll hand it over."

"I sure do like the idea of being a spy," said Buddy. "I could use that kind of excitement in my life right now. Life has been kind of on the stale side lately."

Big Ben, on the hard-of-hearing end of the scale, bellowed, "What's that?"

"I said life was boring," hollered Buddy.

Morty snorted. "I doubt that. You've got a lady friend."

"Well, that's right. But it seems like we do the same stuff all the time. Wave at cars on the front porch. Eat the free samples at the Costco. Go to the early bird specials at the cafeteria." Buddy shrugged. "We're in a rut."

"What you need to do," said Morty, jabbing his finger in the air, "is to shake things up a little bit."

Buddy made a face. "Sure, that all sounds like a wonderful idea. But you know how it is when you get into a rut. In some ways it's sorta comfortable there. It takes a bunch of effort to mess with a routine. Bunches of effort. And I'm an old guy."

"It doesn't have to take too much effort," said Lulu. "Our Derrick squired Peggy Sue's granddaughter around the festival. You should see if Leticia would join you later after you're done cooking. Y'all don't go to festivals every day, after all. And there's stuff to see here—food to eat, people to stare at. I think you could have a fun time."

"Maybe," said Buddy in a considering voice. "Of course, that would involve calling Ms. Swinger on the phone. And I forgot to bring one today."

Morty immediately held out his phone to him. He shrugged. "Okay, okay, y'all. I guess I can try something different. I'll give her a call once I've put in some cooking time."

Morty, Big Ben, and Buddy walked next door, and after a few minutes they returned with Brody, who came over to join Lulu and the Graces. Brody's eyes were tired, his clothes were rumpled, and he generally looked like he'd been through the wringer. "Hi, y'all," he ventured. "Guess you didn't know what you were getting into when you ended up with a booth next to my team."

They gave him a hug. Lulu said, "Brody, it's not your fault. This all has been a nightmare for you, I know."

He nodded, drawing in a deep breath. "I know Reuben and I were fighting with each other yesterday. But we used to be close friends. I hate that this has happened to him."

Cherry said, "Want to have a seat, Brody?" She gestured at a table with her spatula. "I'm going to take a break myself."

"I'll watch the grill," said Flo. "And I'll add that I'll be ready to see the end of the barbequing, too!"

Brody smiled, then suddenly got serious. "One of the reasons I came by is to thank y'all. You've been a really good friend to us, regardless of how everything started out with that big argument between us and Reuben. I can't tell you how much I appreciate that we've got extra hands helping us out right now, for one."

Lulu waved her hands dismissively. "Well, that's nothing to do with us. Morty, Buddy, and Big Ben are the helpful ones."

"We'd never have known them if it hadn't been for you, though," said Brody. "You've got real decent friends."

"I'll second that," said Cherry, holding up her beer. "To friends!"

They toasted friendship and then Brody continued,

"You've been super nice to Sharon, too. You probably don't know how upset this whole situation has made her. First she was upset by Reuben's behavior, which had changed so radically. Then, of course, she was upset right after that by the fact that Reuben ended up dead and that she and I are suspects . . . it's been a nightmare. You've been great friends to her and really talked her off the cliff a couple of times when she felt down over everything. Thanks."

"We're happy to do it, Brody. Y'all have been in a real tough spot," said Cherry.

"So have you, though. You'd never have been mixed up in a murder investigation if it hadn't been for us," said Brody.

Cherry looked at Lulu and gave a half-smile. "Well, I'm not so sure about that."

Brody raised his eyebrows and said, "It's true, then? Sharon said that Flo told her that Lulu has investigated murders before and been able to solve them before the police do."

"I do have a nasty habit of getting involved with murders, yes," said Lulu. "I try to pitch in and help get to the bottom of things. I'm sort of tidying up and putting everything back to normal."

Brody leaned forward and studied her intently. "Then there's something you should know about. I've got to tell your police officer friend, too. Reuben's ex-wife and his teenage son are here at the festival."

"You've seen them walking around?" asked Lulu.

Brody shook his head. "I've seen them at a booth. They're part of a team at the festival. What's more, I've seen the ex-wife hanging around not far from our booth and watching it. Maybe they've been up to something."

"Let's tell Pink. He will be sure to talk to the ex," said Cherry. "It might not be immediate, but he'll get around to it. An ex-wife has got to be on the list of suspects, especially if she was at the festival where it happened."

Brody seemed like he wanted to say more, but at that point they heard Morty's voice calling him, searching for equipment. He thanked them for the drink and headed back over to his booth, leaving the women staring after him.

"What do you think?" asked Cherry in a low voice. "Could the ex have done it?"

Flo snorted. "The ex always *wants* to do it. But how many actually act on it? Maybe our friend Brody wants to focus attention on someone else for a change. He's got to know that he's a main suspect, considering he was in a huge fight with the victim a few hours before he showed up dead."

"Yeah," said Cherry glumly, staring into her empty beer bottle, "but that also describes me, too."

Lulu said, "I think we've just increased our suspects by one. Maybe by two, depending on this teenager. Is Reuben's child nineteen or thirteen? If he's older, maybe he felt resentful and did it himself. Which would be a very sad thing."

"Even kids have been homicidal," reminded Flo, absently patting her beehive hairdo.

"Sure, but not very often," said Cherry. "We should find out more about those two."

"And more about John and Tim the waiter," said Lulu with a sigh. She filled them in on what Derrick and the girls had shared with her. "We have our work cut out for us."

"Where should we start?" asked Cherry.

"Where should I start, you mean?" asked Lulu ruefully. "*You* need to be getting your samples out for the judges. I believe I'll help close down the restaurant tonight and give Ben and Sara a break."

Cherry said, "And ask Tim a few questions while you're there, I'm guessing?"

"Exactly. I won't have a chance otherwise. I can't pull a waiter aside when the restaurant is as busy as it is," said Lulu. "We'd have another murder on our hands then because Ben and Sara would have my head."

Even after closing, there was still a very busy feel to Aunt Pat's. The staff swept and vacuumed, removed tablecloths, and wiped down tables. Ben was cleaning in the kitchen and Sara was working on the books in the office. They both looked beat.

"Why don't y'all go ahead and scoot on off home," said Lulu to Sara. "I can finish up the accounts and the kitchen in a jiff."

Sara frowned. "Are you sure? You're spending a heap of time at the festival, and I know you took the girls around today. Don't you want to go turn in yourself?"

"You know, I kind of miss my Aunt Pat's time. It's hard to go from spending all day here to no time here at all. No, y'all go on home and I'll lock up. Give the twins and Derrick a kiss for me," said Lulu.

Sara wasn't going to argue with her, especially as worn out as she was. She quickly collected her pocketbook and Ben, and they left in a hurry.

Most of the staff was leaving, too, so Lulu was quick to pull Tim aside before he made his way to the parking deck. "Tim, can I talk to you for a few minutes in the office?"

He followed her in and sat at the table in the room. "I'm sorry—did I do something wrong?"

Lulu quickly shook her head. Tim Gentry's face had a perennially anxious expression on it, and she didn't want to make it any worse. He had very dark hair that appeared dyed to her, as if the worry had turned him gray prematurely. He was lean, almost gaunt.

"No," Lulu said, "you've been a great worker since you've joined us, Tim. I guess that's been . . . let's see . . ."

"About four months," said Tim. "And I'm grateful for the job," he added quickly, again getting that strained crease around his lips.

Lulu quickly got to the point to avoid making the man any more anxious. "I was curious about a connection of yours, actually—someone we saw you with recently that we didn't know you knew. A man named Reuben Shaw."

What little remaining color in Tim's face quickly vanished and his shoulders slumped as if the name itself was a burden. "What?" he mumbled. "How did you . . ."

"We saw you at the festival talking to him," said Lulu. "Or arguing with him, really. I wanted to find out how you knew him." She leaned forward and put her hand on Tim's arm. "We're a family here at Aunt Pat's, Tim. I look after my own and you're one of mine. My Ella Beth thinks the sun rises and sets with you because you play Crazy Eights with her. If I can help you, I will. But I need to know what's going on."

Tim nodded slowly. "That family feeling is real strong here, and I've gotten to love my time at Aunt Pat's. I'll tell you about me and Reuben, Mrs. Taylor. I don't understand why you're interested in it, though." His gray eyes gazed questioningly at her.

"Please call me Lulu, Tim. And the reason why I'm interested is because Reuben is dead," she said gently. "In fact, he was murdered last night."

Tim put his hands to his face and covered his eyes with his long fingers. He stayed that way for almost a minute, digesting the information. Finally, he put his hands down and looked at Lulu with worried eyes. "I didn't know. I didn't know anything about that."

"I know," said Lulu soothingly. "It's got to come as a shock to you. How did you know Reuben?"

"I've been friends with Reuben for the last few years," he said slowly. "Reuben is some years older than me, but we got to know each other because our wives worked together at a preschool. After a while, we started doing things as couples. We had a lot of things in common. I was involved in construction, too, but because I'm an accountant."

Lulu couldn't help wondering why an accountant would be a full-time waiter at her restaurant. Maybe he should be doing their books for them instead of Sara or her doing them.

Lulu said, "It sounded like Reuben was upset with you at the festival. He seemed feisty most of yesterday, but I wonder why he was talking in a very loud voice with you." She didn't want to bring the girls or Derrick into the conversation—she decided to let Tim think that she was the one who'd overheard the argument.

She thought she saw a flash of fear in Tim's eyes. Then he said, "Reuben was upset, yes ma'am. Lately, Reuben was almost always upset, over everything. I can't believe he couldn't understand why I wasn't returning his messages." But Tim couldn't seem to look Lulu in the eye. He was hiding something, she was sure of it.

Clearly, though, he wasn't ready to talk about it.

"I hear that Reuben acted upset with everyone," said Lulu. "But I understand he wasn't always like that—that he was fun to be around at one point. But before he died, he even got into an argument with our Cherry. He couldn't seem to be around anyone without turning it into a huge scene. Do you know when he started being like that and why it happened?"

This time Tim didn't only turn pale, he was tinged with green, and Lulu wondered if she needed to grab the trash can real quick just in case. She had no idea that was such a loaded question.

Tim shook his head again. "I sure don't," he said, still not meeting Lulu's eyes.

The next day, Lulu was back at the festival. She'd never spent so much time at Rock and Ribs in all her days. The barbeque contest had been judged by the time she arrived and she was sorry to hear that the Graces hadn't won. But she couldn't be too surprised. After all, there had been plenty of distractions for the women to contend with. And there were over three hundred other competitors there—most of which were one hundred percent focused on cooking.

"Pooh," said Cherry when they were all sitting around a table in the booth. "I thought we might have at least gotten some sort of prize. Our barbeque is really good . . . not like some people's."

"Oh, well," said Evelyn philosophically. "There's always next year."

"If we want to participate next year," grumbled Cherry. "This year has been kind of crazy."

"There's not usually murders at the festival," reminded Flo. "And next year we'll be a lot more prepared since we'll have done it before."

"I guess," said Cherry glumly. Then she glanced over Flo's shoulder and raised her eyebrows. "Hi there—can we help you with something?"

There was a woman standing there with a tall boy. The woman was pretty big, a problem that wasn't helped by the large paisley print on her dress. The boy dwarfed her in height but clearly appeared uncomfortable where the woman seemed confrontational.

"I'm looking for Cherry and Lulu," the woman said in a rasping voice that hinted at cigarette smoke.

"You've found them," said Cherry, crossing her arms as if ready to do battle. This woman didn't seem particularly friendly.

"I'm Dawn Brown and this is my son, Finn Shaw."

She almost acted like she expected them to know who they were. And after studying Finn for a moment, Lulu thought she might. "Oh. You must be Reuben's son and his . . . wife."

"Ex-wife," Dawn said briskly. "We wanted to talk to y'all for a little while . . . seeing as how you found Reuben's body and all."

The woman didn't seem to be making any concession for the fact that Finn was there. You'd think that she'd be softening her words around her son. Even though she still clearly had hard feelings for Reuben, his son might not share them. It was his father who'd been killed, after all.

They invited Dawn and Finn to take a seat and offered them food, which they turned down, and soft drinks, which they took them up on. Once they were settled, Dawn said, "The police were talking to us about what happened. Y'all were over in the booth next door and were messing around in Reuben's storage area? The police were telling us about it and it didn't sound right to me."

Lulu sighed. It didn't, when you put it that way. It made it sound like she and Cherry had been snooping around. Or even worse, like they were possibly responsible somehow for what happened. "We were. I know that sounds funny, but we were searching for a missing tarp that I wanted to hold over my head while I ran through the rain for the parking lot. We'd seen a lot of tarps coming and going next door, and Cherry said that the things for our booth and the things for Reuben's booth were right next to each other when they were putting the booths together."

Cherry nodded. "We thought they might have accidentally taken one of our tarps, so we walked over to the storage area to see if we could find it."

Or that Reuben had snatched one of their tarps to try to make trouble. And at that point they didn't really know much about Sharon and Brody and what kind of people they were, either.

Dawn nodded like it made better sense to her. Maybe she was thinking that Reuben might have taken the tarp, too. "And he'd been stabbed," she said in a conversational tone.

Lulu and Cherry both winced, thinking of Finn. The boy simply seemed tired, though—the harsh words didn't cause him any change of expression.

"I'm afraid so," said Lulu quietly. "It was a really terrible evening. We're very sorry," she said.

"Don't feel sorry on my account," said Dawn, waving a dismissive hand. "There were plenty of times when I'd have liked to have killed the man myself. Especially since he wasn't pulling his weight with Finn."

This uncomfortable conversation was abruptly interrupted when Ella Beth and Coco came racing into the booth. "The Graces should have won!" said Coco.

"Y'all had the best ribs here," said Ella Beth loyally.

Flo and Evelyn gave the girls a hug and Cherry said, "Aren't y'all sweet for saying so! Are you doing one more walk-through today?"

"Where's Derrick?" asked Lulu.

Derrick came in, much slower-paced than the twins had. "Here I am," he said. "Guess I don't have quite as much energy as Coco and Ella Beth. We were checking in and saying hi." He gazed curiously at Dawn and Finn, and Lulu quickly made introductions.

"What are y'all planning on doing?" asked Lulu.

"We're going to check out all the different booths,"

said Ella Beth. "There was one that we saw when we were with Flo that we wanted to show Derrick. It was a triple-decker with a white picket fence with pinwheels stuck in it that sort of resembled a clubhouse. Then there was a booth where you could make crafts, so we thought we'd go by there. And the main stage has bluegrass music playing now, and is going to have a rock band a little later. We also were going to get some cotton candy because Coco said she was dying for some."

"Blue cotton candy," said Coco.

Finn was wistful as Ella Beth listed their plans. Despite his height, he was very boyish with gangling arms and legs that he didn't seem to know what to do with. "Finn," said Lulu, "have you had a chance to walk around the festival at all? Get a feel for it? It's really a lot of fun—good food, interesting people."

Finn shook his head, but watched his mother cautiously, as if not sure if he should admit that he'd been at the festival but not really explored it.

"Why don't you go with Derrick and the girls for a while? Sounds like they're going to go have fun. Might be a good chance for you to see what it's all about," said Lulu.

"And eat cotton candy!" said Ella Beth.

Finn gave his mother a hopeful look.

Derrick said, "Sure, that's fine, if he wants to hang out with us." He cast his eyes down, a little shy, but Ella Beth and Coco were already chiming in. "We can show you the best places to get food here," said Ella Beth. "And where there's some fun stuff to do," said Coco. Clearly, they were going to be competing with each other to see who could show Finn the festival better.

After Finn left with the kids, Dawn stared after him for a moment. Then she gritted, "I guess I should feel sorrier than I do. About Reuben's death." She cleared her throat and stared at the temporary flooring that made up the bottom of the Graces' booth. "He did give me a beautiful son. We had some good years and good times together."

The bitterness was never very far away, though. "The reason I sound so uncaring is because he basically abandoned us. He changed overnight. Next thing I knew, I was searching for a place to work . . . because I wasn't going to be able to make it as a preschool teacher single mom. He never did send along the child support he was supposed to. How was Finn going to go to college on *my* salary?"

She dropped into a brooding silence and the other women gazed uncomfortably at each other. Lulu said, "That's real hard, Dawn. But Finn seems to be a fine young man, so you must be doing something right."

Dawn's small eyes gazed at her blankly as if unable to see where she could possibly have done something right. "Well, that's what we call a miracle," she said finally, "because between Reuben and me, I'd say we'd messed that boy up."

Flo said, "Were you able to end up finding a job and keep your head above water, then?" It was said in the tone of someone who really wanted to know how the story ended. Flo had gone through tough times of her own, and she was a sucker for an inspirational story.

"I found a job, but I wasn't really qualified to *do* anything. Ended up working a few part-time jobs. No benefits and I've got health problems, so it's been real rough. Rough on Finn, too. Wouldn't have been so bad if Reuben had helped us out some."

"This might sound crass," said Lulu, slowly trying to think through her words before saying them, "but do you think . . . well, the will . . ."

"Do I think that we might get money from Reuben's will? I'd be surprised if he even had a will at all. That's one guy who thought so much of himself that I bet he never thought he would actually die. My grandpa never had a will, either, and when he passed, his estate had to go through probate court—which was a nightmare for my mama. I bet it'll be the same thing for Reuben. After it makes its way through court, there won't be much of his 'estate' left—but maybe Finn will at least get something."

"Having a booth at the festival is pretty expensive," said Evelyn. "If Reuben didn't have a lot of money, how would he have managed it?"

Dawn shrugged. "How would I know? I guess he either charged it to a credit card or the other teammates footed the bill."

Lulu said, "You mentioned that Reuben changed overnight. Do you know what made him change? Was it really overnight?" This wasn't the first time she'd heard that Reuben had turned into a different person in a short period of time.

"It really, literally was overnight. One day he was fine and dandy. We even went out with friends that evening. The next day, he wouldn't look me in the eye and everything started going downhill from that." Dawn shrugged. "I figured he must have met a woman when he was out that night. Why else would he change that much and that quick? But I never have seen or heard of another woman spending time with Reuben. Maybe it didn't end up working out for him. I hope it didn't. Maybe she messed up his heart like he messed up mine."

"How did y'all end up at the festival?" asked Cherry. "Did you know that Reuben was going to be here?"

"The head of the preschool where I work has a booth—he has one every year. He likes to have a lot of team members so that one person isn't spending all their time cooking. He was kind of pressuring us all to sign up, so I went ahead and did it, and signed Finn up, too. Lately, it seemed like we weren't doing any fun stuff at all, so I thought it would be a good way to do something different. I didn't know Reuben would have a booth here, too."

"Is that something he usually did?" asked Flo.

"Not at all. He'd talked about doing it for years, but it

never happened. Sometimes, during happier times, we'd come to Rock and Ribs together and we'd sample the food at different booths . . . Reuben always managed to get us an invite into booths. When he wanted to be, he could be real charming. But after we'd taste the food, Reuben would always be scornful about it—not in front of the people who gave it to us, of course. As soon as we left, though, he'd be saying how much better his own ribs were or his own special sauce. Reuben could really brag, and he was very competitive. He was a good cook, too. I guess this year he finally decided to enter," said Dawn.

"Did you run into him here?" asked Lulu.

"I didn't. Too bad, because I'd have been able to give him a piece of my mind. He wasn't real good about returning the messages I left on his machine. The police, of course, were interested to hear where I was when he was killed. It wasn't our shift, so Finn and I were taking in the festival and all the booths," said Dawn. "Too bad for us. Now we don't have an alibi except for what we can give each other."

"Well, I guess I should be heading back. I'm supposed to help with the booth cleanup now that the festival is wrapping up. Seeing as how it's my boss, I'm trying to be especially helpful." Dawn gave a pained smile to show that she didn't really feel like being helpful. "Do you mind sending Finn to our booth when he comes back? Thanks for offering to have your kids take him around. He doesn't get to do much that's fun."

After Dawn left, Cherry said, "What do you make of all that, Lulu? She sure is a sourpuss, isn't she?"

"I guess she has reason to be. It sounds like Reuben really gave her a rough time—especially with her being sick and all. And with trying to raise a son all by herself," said Lulu.

"Do you think she could have done it?" asked Flo.

"Why would she have, though?" asked Evelyn. "What would she get out of it? She said that the man didn't have any money. And if he was dead, he wouldn't have the opportunity to start working again and make the money she needed to get for child support. It sounds to me like Reuben was worth more alive than dead to her."

"Unless that bitterness of hers caused her to lash out at him. The need for revenge can be a powerful thing," said Lulu.

"Now we know she had the opportunity to do it," said Cherry. "And she had the motive to do it, too—she clearly couldn't stand the guy."

"So what's left?" asked Flo. "Motive, opportunity . . ."

"And means," said Lulu with a sigh. "I'm thinking that getting her hands on a butcher knife at a barbeque competition wouldn't have been hard for Dawn at all."

Chapter 7

About forty-five minutes later, Finn did come back with the kids. He was a lot more relaxed than he had when he left, although his eyes quickly clouded with worry when he asked where his mom was.

"She's headed back to your booth to help clean up," said Lulu. Then she added gently, "The last couple of days must have been really hard on you."

Lulu saw Finn's lower lip tremble for half a second before he steeled himself again. "Yeah. It's been harder than I'd have thought it would be. Of course, Mom says Dad totally shafted us and we shouldn't care that he's gone." But his words came across more as a question than a statement.

Cherry said stoutly, "Well, of course you're going

to be sad about your dad. He was your *dad*, no matter what."

"And you shouldn't feel disloyal to your mom for feeling that way," said Lulu.

Finn smiled gratefully at them. "Thanks," he said gruffly.

Finn shifted, and Lulu was trying to think of a way to change the subject when Morty came over from the booth next door. Ella Beth and Coco, who had busily been telling the Graces about their time wandering around the festival, ran over to give Morty a hug. "Whoa!" said Morty, taking a couple of exaggerated steps backward. "You girls have gotten so big that you're gonna topple this old guy over. What's your mama feeding y'all? You're growing like weeds!"

"Lots of barbeque, I think," said Lulu with a smile.

"And you've got a new young man with you, too?" asked Morty.

"His name is Finn. We showed him all around the festival," said Coco.

"And we ate cotton candy," said Ella Beth.

"Indeed you did! I see cotton candy stickiness right there on your sleeve," said Morty.

"Morty is a musician," said Lulu to Finn. "He sings and plays several different instruments."

"Most notably the trumpet," said Evelyn. "Morty can sure play some trumpet."

Finn's eyes lit up. "I play the trumpet, too. Not great,

but I'm trying. Mom can't afford lessons and I can't get them at school because I'm too old to start an instrument in the high school's music program."

"Why don't you come by Aunt Pat's restaurant after school on Monday or Tuesday and I can give you some tips?" said Morty. He took on an expression of false modesty. "Not that I'm the best trumpet player of all time or anything . . ."

"Very nearly!" said Lulu loyally.

"But I'd be delighted to share my knowledge with the next generation. I had lots of folks helping me on my way to being a musician. It would be nice to sort of pay them back."

Finn said eagerly, "That would be awesome. I'm sure I could come by next week. Thanks, Morty." There was a spring in his step as he took off to meet back up with his mom.

Lulu was about ready to head back to Aunt Pat's when Brody stuck his head around the side of the Graces' booth. "Hey there. Okay if I take a break from taking the booth down and talk to y'all for a minute or two? I know our conversation got cut short earlier."

"Sure thing," said Cherry. "I'm about ready to take a break myself."

The chairs hadn't been packed up yet so Brody dropped down into one in relief at getting off his feet.

He said, "I know I thanked y'all for being friendly to Sharon. She's been so stressed out about the way Reuben was acting and then the murder—you've really helped her out by listening to her and just being there."

"We're happy to do it," said Cherry. "Sharon is a great person."

Brody said, "I was wondering if maybe you could keep on being her friend. Now that the festival is over, even. You might not know this, because I don't know if we mentioned it, but we recently moved to Memphis. Sharon doesn't know a soul here but me, and of course I'm working most of the time."

"You just moved here?" echoed Lulu in surprise. "But y'all knew Reuben so well."

"That's only because I've known Reuben Shaw for ages. He and I went to college together and kept in touch pretty well. We didn't see each other much, but once every summer, we'd go on a trip together—just guys. Sometimes we'd go hunting, sometimes fishing. Sometimes we'd even do stuff like skydiving. That's how I kept up with Reuben and what was going on with his life, and how he kept up with me."

"What made you finally decide to move here?" asked Cherry.

"Well, I'd been at a bank in Atlanta for ages, but then they made a lot of cuts and I didn't have a job. Since they'd made big cuts, there were a lot of other folks in my shoes, looking for a banking job in Atlanta. When I couldn't find anything for a while, I called Reuben up. I thought he was still his old self, from the way he got right on it. He scouted around and found me a job in Memphis."

Lulu said, "He knew people in banking?" It didn't seem to jibe with Reuben's background.

"He did, actually. Reuben had worked on tons of homes as a contractor. He knew some very wealthy and connected people. Before I knew it, he'd set me up an interview. When the bank made me an offer, we moved right over," said Brody.

Lulu said, "You mentioned that you thought Reuben was his old self. But he wasn't?"

Brody shook his head. "That got real clear, real fast. He did help Sharon and me with moving in and gave us advice on where to buy a house in the area. But after that, it seemed like whatever demons were chasing him had finally caught up with him. Of course, Sharon and I had known that he'd gotten divorced—we'd talked on the phone about it when it was going on and I'd offered to come to Memphis to support him. He didn't want me to come, though—acted like it was something that he wanted to deal with himself."

"The divorce seemed to really affect him?" asked Lulu.

Brody shrugged. "I guess it was the divorce. Something really affected him, but not being in town at the time, I don't know what it was. It must have been something big. I figured that he either felt real guilty about his own part in the divorce or else he missed Dawn and Finn more than he'd thought he would."

"Dawn and Finn actually came by to talk to us," offered Cherry. "She wanted to hear from us about discovering Reuben's body. She was saying that he hadn't been treating them right since the divorce. She thought he wasn't sending them enough money."

Lulu said, "Or *any* money, maybe."

"That's the thing, though," said Brody. "I don't know how much money he even had. I'm not saying that he didn't treat Dawn and Finn wrong, because it sounds like he did. But when Sharon and I moved to Memphis, I could tell that his business was off. And the person Reuben contacted to get me a job was asking me about Reuben, too."

"What did he say?" asked Lulu.

Brody said, "He was saying that Reuben had been a top-notch contractor for him and he couldn't have been more pleased. But he wasn't sure he'd hire him today if he needed work done. He'd heard a bunch of people talking about Reuben, and the Better Business Bureau was poking around, too. I could tell that Reuben had started drinking a lot and wasn't going to work most days. But I didn't know if it was because he didn't have any jobs or whether he was being lazy and not going to the jobs that he had."

"So his customers weren't happy with him," said Lulu.

"Not a bit. They said he was using shoddy material . . . real cheap stuff . . . to cut corners. And he wasn't showing up on the site or hitting his deadlines. Sometimes their kitchen would be in total ruins and there was no end in sight—he wouldn't have even placed the order for the counters or the cabinets that the homeowner had decided on," said Brody.

"So maybe he wasn't bringing much money in, after all," said Cherry. "Although that probably wouldn't have satisfied his ex-wife. She's working a bunch of part-time jobs apparently, to make ends meet."

"She wasn't real sympathetic, no," said Brody. "Reuben said she was after him all the time to send them money. Called him a deadbeat dad, that kind of thing. Said if he'd get his rear end out of bed and go work that then he'd be able to help them out."

"Sounds like a reasonable assumption," drawled Flo.

Lulu said, "Sharon talked about one customer who was really harping on Reuben—actually, it was someone who'd been hanging out with us here at the booth. His name was John."

Brody's eyes widened. "Why didn't Sharon tell me this? He was here at the festival? And that close to Reuben without killing him?"

"I guess that remains to be seen," said Lulu, rather worried. "What's the story there? Did you know anything about it? How did Sharon know, since y'all haven't been in town that long?"

"Even though Reuben had been acting out, we'd still try to be friendly. We didn't know what was causing him to behave the way he was, but he and I had been friends for so many years that I was still reaching out to him. After all, he'd even helped find me a job here. I'd go by after work and visit Reuben—try to snap him out of his funk sometimes. Without any luck, of course. But one time Sharon and I were over there—Sharon had doubled a recipe and we took it over to Reuben for supper so he wouldn't be eating Beanee Weenees that night—and we saw Reuben screaming at this man at his door. Really screaming at him."

Brody stopped for a moment, remembering. "I'd never seen Reuben like that. He was mad. Like he was the other day at the booth. Furious."

"Why was he so mad when it sounds like it was the customer who should have been mad at him instead?" asked Lulu.

"The customer was furious at him," said Brody. "He had a knife in his hand as a matter of fact. But the guy was that icy kind of mad. Scary. Very, very calm, very measured kind of voice. The way he was talking to Reuben was cutting. He basically said that Reuben was totally incompetent at his job—that he was the worst contractor ever. That's the kind of thing that really got Reuben's goat. You saw how competitive he was. It made Reuben flip out."

"And this guy was John? The man who was over at our booth?" asked Cherry, eyes opening wide.

"He must have been. I mean, I didn't see him or anything, but Sharon would have recognized him. He's the only dissatisfied customer that we knew about," said Brody.

Lulu realized she'd been holding her breath. She inhaled and said, "What happened after that? Since John had a knife and everything, it seems like it could really have gotten ugly."

"The guy—John, I guess—backed off when he saw me coming up to him and saw Sharon sitting in the car. He must have realized he didn't need any witnesses. Reuben wasn't exactly being reasonable at this point, so I was the one who told John that it was time for him to leave. He'd already shoved the knife in his pocket, so I grabbed him real firm by the arm and marched him off to his car."

"Did Reuben say anything about John or what had happened after John had finally left?" asked Lulu, leaning forward and listening intently.

"Not a whole lot. But he did say that he was the angriest customer he'd ever had and that he wouldn't leave him alone—he was always getting phone calls and e-mails and texts from the guy about finishing his house." Brody shrugged again.

Lulu and Cherry exchanged a glance. "Doesn't it seem like a coincidence that the same fellow would show up at our tent? Right next door to Reuben's? And that he would cut out of there as soon as he thought he might be recognized?" asked Cherry.

"Life is full of coincidences," said Lulu. "But this one does seem suspect, doesn't it?"

Brody said, "What do you think he was doing? He knew that Reuben's booth was next door, didn't he?"

"I think he did know that Reuben was next door," said Lulu. "But to find out what he was doing requires us talking to John about it." She paused, then asked Brody, "One more question. Did y'all put up all the money for your booth? Or did Reuben? And if Reuben did, where did he get the money?"

Brody flushed. "Well, that's a good question. And what I told you was totally correct—Reuben didn't seem like he had much money. In fact, he'd borrowed some from us, once or twice. When he was signing us up in March for the festival, he sure seemed like he was broke. I figured maybe he was putting the registration costs and other stuff on a credit card. But the last couple of weeks, he seemed to have come into some money somehow. His annoying behavior has stressed me out to the point where I didn't want to give him an opportunity to brag, so I didn't ask him about it. Maybe Sharon knows. She talked to him more than I did in the days leading up to the festival."

"We'll ask her later," said Lulu. "And don't worry—we'd love to keep Sharon as a friend."

Lulu helped clean up the booth as much as she could before the Graces shooed her away. "This is our mess, so *we'll* clean it up," said Evelyn, far more industrious about cleaning than she ever had about the cooking.

"Besides," said Flo with a sigh, "there's more rain

coming over, according to the radar. You may want to get out of here before you turn into a Mud Person like we're sure to be."

So Lulu drove back to the restaurant. Now that the barbeque festival was over, it had slowed down at Aunt Pat's, too. She knew she should feel sorry about that, but the truth was that the restaurant was still plenty busy . . . and she was wanting a spot to sit and be quiet and think things through for a few minutes.

She rocked on the front porch and greeted diners as they came in. The Labs, B. B. and Elvis, were on the porch, once again snoozing in the afternoon heat and not even bothering to lift their heads when people came and left.

Then sometime, and she wasn't sure exactly when, she apparently dropped off to sleep in the rocking chair. The combination of the buzzing fans, the snoring of the Labs, and the white noise of conversation drifting from the dining room helped her nod off.

The sound of torrential rain woke her up with a start and for a moment she wasn't sure where she was or what time of day it was. Then Sara poked her head around the porch door and smiled when she saw that her mother-in-law was waking up. "You must be worn out to be able to sleep with everyone stomping through the porch," said Sara.

Lulu laughed and rubbed her eyes, "I guess so. I wouldn't have said I was that tired, but all the excitement must have taken its toll on me. How are things going here? And what time is it?"

"I'm fixing to head out, as a matter of fact . . . but don't worry, it's early. We're still in the middle of the dinner rush. We have enough help for the rest of the evening and it's slowed down some," said Sara.

Lulu said, "That's good. You've spent enough time at Aunt Pat's the last few days. We all need a break. And I know the girls will be glad to have you home. Derrick, too."

Sara smiled. "You know you've been away for a while when even a teenager is happy to have you around!"

"Before you head out," said Lulu in a low voice, glancing swiftly around her, "I was wondering if I could ask you about something real quick."

Chapter

8

Sara perched on the edge of a rocker. "Sure thing."

"It's Tim, one of our waiters," said Lulu, eyes still on the door, in case he suddenly popped out.

Sara nodded. "I know which guy you're talking about. He's not here, by the way, so you don't have to worry about him overhearing us. He worked the morning and lunch shift today."

"Oh good. What do you think about Tim?" asked Lulu.

"He's been a real good waiter. That's my opinion anyway. We can depend on him to be here and he works hard while he's here. He even plays cards with the girls sometimes," said Sara.

"So Ella Beth told me," said Lulu with a smile.

Sara stared thoughtfully into space for a moment. "Lately, though, he's been kind of stressed."

"I thought he always seemed stressed," said Lulu.

"He does tend to sport that I've-been-run-over-by-a-bus look," agreed Sara. "Still, it's been more obvious lately."

Lulu said, "No idea what's bothering him? Does he ever talk about his personal life?"

"Never. One thing that was odd yesterday, though, come to think of it. He was in the office . . . which isn't a big deal, of course, since it's like an employee break room, too. But the strange part was that he was on the computer."

Lulu frowned. "Hmm. That is sort of unusual, isn't it? Maybe he was checking his e-mail or something."

"Maybe. But when he spotted me, he jumped a mile and his face turned bright red. It struck me as a guilty reaction. I think he's probably hiding something, Lulu."

Cherry hooted on her end of the phone, making Lulu wince on hers. "Woo-hoo! A stakeout! Lulu, this is what I've always dreamed of."

"Well, I guess it's not *really* a stakeout. For a real stakeout, you want to be hidden the whole time," said Lulu.

"We don't want to be seen, do we? That's why you're

saying we're going to park down the road from John's house and lay low," said Cherry.

"Right. But all we're doing is waiting for John to come out of his house and into his driveway so we can talk to him alone," said Lulu.

"Remind me again why we're not knocking on his door and going in to talk to him?" asked Cherry.

"Safety first," said Lulu. "We don't want John to kill us in his foyer, remember?"

"Oh, that's right. Although I guess we could pack heat and go over there. Or take Pink with us," said Cherry.

"This way will probably work better—I hope anyway. If it doesn't, we can always go to plan B. Bring something to do while we wait. It might be boring," said Lulu.

This was how they ended up down the street from John's house with Cherry wearing huge sunglasses that took up her entire face and a fuchsia scarf covering her hair. "Is that scarf less noticeable than your hair would be?" asked Lulu doubtfully.

"Sure it is! Besides, I couldn't pass up the chance to wear a disguise during our stakeout."

Cherry had been pretty keyed up at first, despite the fact that it was very early in the morning. Mighty early. They'd decided that they knew that John would be heading out to work in the morning and it would take less time to wait for him on his way out the door to work than to wait for him to come home from there.

Still, though, it did take a while. Cherry's stomach

growled and she said, "I guess you don't have breakfast for us in that huge pocketbook of yours?"

Lulu rummaged through it. "Not breakfast, but I have a few granola bars. And bottled waters. And I always keep treats for the Labs in here. B. B. and Elvis love to see me coming because they know they'll get a tasty treat."

Cherry chuckled as she took them from her, "You must have been a Girl Scout, Lulu, because you surely are prepared."

Lulu was deep into her sudoku and Cherry was falling asleep and jerking back awake repeatedly when she suddenly sat up straight and put her face against the car window. "There he is! There's John."

And it was. He was very mild-mannered and non-threatening in khaki pants and a striped golf shirt with a still-sleepy expression on his face.

"Let's go!" said Cherry, reaching for the car door and struggling unsuccessfully with it. "Oy! Lulu, you've got the locks on."

"Well, safety first," said Lulu again, unlocking the car doors and hurrying to keep up with Cherry, who'd already sprung out of the car and was fairly sprinting up to a startled John in his driveway.

"Hi there, ladies," said John, smiling, but with wary eyes. "I wasn't expecting to see you here." He raised his eyebrows at Cherry's scarf and sunglasses.

Lulu said, "Actually, we tried to find you at the festival, John. But your teammates said that you weren't there anymore. They gave us your address when they realized we wanted to talk to you."

"What's this all about?" His tone was still pleasant, but now the wariness was trickling through into his voice.

Cherry said, gazing at John through narrowed eyes, "That's what we'd like to hear, too. We thought that you didn't know Reuben."

"I didn't *know* him," said John stiffly. "He's not the kind of person that I'd know."

"All right then," said Cherry, reflecting John's snippy tone back at him, "*acquainted* with him. You let us think that you didn't know who Reuben Shaw was."

"And, in fact," said Lulu gently, feeling like she and Cherry were playing good cop/bad cop, "You did know who he was. And I believe you were at the Graces' booth because you were wanting to confront Reuben."

John's hands shook with some kind of strong emotion. He shoved them into his pockets, his keys rattling as he did. He turned slightly and gazed broodingly at his house, a suburban two-story brick. "Seeing my house from the outside," he said, "you'd never guess how totally devastated it is on the inside. How the kitchen is barely functional. How the master bathroom is gutted and cave-like. Looking at me, you'd never know how much money I've sunk into this totally unfinished project. Money that I didn't even have to sink."

John's voice, although quiet, was chock-full of rage. Lulu and Cherry glanced at each other. Was John going to flip out here in his driveway? Lulu said, "That must have been incredibly frustrating for you . . ."

He gave a short laugh. "Frustrating? Infuriating. And you're talking like it's in the past tense. It's not. I've been living practically like an animal in there for months and months. At one point, I didn't even have any working plumbing. The kitchen had no electricity. And this guy, this Reuben, wouldn't even return my calls."

Cherry's eyes were wide. "I'd want to string him up. I really would."

John didn't even seem to register that she'd spoken. "I'd be expecting for him and his crew to show up and get me out of this mess. To make some kind of progress. Sometimes, on those rare occasions when I did manage to get him on the phone, he'd be so incredibly slick. He'd promise to be there. Oh, we were waiting on materials to come in, he'd say. They're being delivered to your house today, he'd claim. But they wouldn't."

Lulu said, "So he'd string you along, promising that construction materials would come in and the crew would be there . . . and nothing?"

"Nothing. I wasn't the only person he was doing this to, either. And I'm a total victim . . . helpless. I don't have the money to even hire someone else to step in and do the job right, let alone to finish it. Reuben wouldn't even answer his phone after a while." John spread out his hands in a hopeless gesture. "What was I supposed to do?"

Lulu said, "So you showed up at the festival. You were already on a team. Maybe with your office, right?"

"Not exactly. More like the brother and friends of someone at my office. I was keen to have a real spot to hang out there. Reuben was such a blabbermouth. No wonder the work that he actually did was so shoddy—he was running his mouth the whole time that he should have been paying attention to what he was doing. Anyway, he was always bragging about how he made the best barbeque and sauce and how he was going to win the barbeque fest with his buddies."

"I'm surprised y'all were even talking to each other," Cherry said. "Sounded like you were ready to kill each other most days."

"Most days we were. But this was before everything started going sour," said John. He was getting worked up again. "Okay, now tell me why I'm getting all these questions. What are you, private investigators?"

Cherry glanced over at Lulu and snickered. Probably trying to picture Lulu in her peach-colored floral print dress as Sam Spade. Then Cherry cleared her throat and said coolly, "In a manner of speaking."

Lulu said, "We're trying to get to the bottom of things. One way we want to do that is to figure out what you were doing at the festival. We didn't realize that you even knew Reuben. And we sure didn't get that impression when you scooted out of there as soon as we heard that fight in Reuben's booth. Why were you were keeping such a close eye on Reuben? What were you trying to accomplish?"

John glanced around him to see if any of his neighbors were paying attention to what they were doing. "What was I trying to accomplish? A couple of different things. Maybe I wasn't thinking one hundred percent clearly—that's what happens when you're completely desperate. The first thing I wanted was my house put back together again, and everything at least working—plumbing, electricity—the basics. I didn't want to have to pay any extra money for that, either. I'd been stupid and paid Reuben up front. Stupid! Why *wouldn't* I have, though? He had the best references in town. He'd worked for all the big bankers, all the CEOs. Everybody thought he'd done such a great job. So I dumped all the money I'd put aside for the project into Reuben's hands right away."

John's eyes glowed with fury, especially when he mentioned his own stupidity. This was clearly a guy who didn't like to mess up. The fact that Reuben had pushed him into making a huge mistake was maybe the biggest reason why John was so upset.

"At this point, the guy wouldn't even talk to me. I knew he was going to be stuck cooking at the festival—what better time to have a captive audience?" asked John, spreading his hands out inquiringly.

"What if he still hadn't talked to you?" asked Lulu.

"What if he ignored you or laughed at you or told you to hire a lawyer?"

"It crossed my mind that maybe I could pick up dirt on him somehow. You know, some kind of leverage against him that I could use to get him to finish up the mess he made. Maybe he was doing drugs, maybe he was having an affair with someone, maybe he was doing something that he wouldn't want people to find out about. It seemed kind of likely to me, actually, since he was the kind of guy that might do stuff he shouldn't do." John shrugged. "Who knows? I wanted to see what I could find out on him or about him. And if I didn't hear anything, I could at least wait for a moment when he was alone to talk to him about my house."

Cherry said, "Surveillance, huh?" in a scornful voice as if she hadn't done the same exact thing outside John's house. "And how did that work out for you?" She had her hands on her hips. Cherry wouldn't like the fact that she'd been tricked by John while he was hanging out with them in the booth. She'd been part of a conspiracy that she hadn't known anything about. Cherry always wanted to know what was going on.

"Not real well, obviously," said John. "I almost blew it by going over to the booth when that fight was going on. I was sure Reuben saw me there. Then, of course, the guy ended up dead so that didn't help me out. Now I'm stuck." The frustration was spilling over into his voice.

"If he's dead, he clearly isn't going to help me put my house back together again."

"Or maybe," said Cherry, still sounding annoyed. "Maybe Reuben *did* see you. Maybe when he was walking around later, he was out searching for you. Reuben was the kind of guy who could get pretty mad and he wouldn't have been happy seeing you at the festival."

"Maybe," said Lulu gently, "when he caught up with you, things got out of control really quickly. You could even have started off trying to be reasonable and Reuben was the one who flew off the handle. It could be that you were even defending yourself from him. Maybe he was the one with the knife."

John backed up. "Hey now. I didn't kill Reuben. Why would I want to? All I wanted to do was to have the guy finish up the work that I'd paid for. If he was dead, I wasn't going to get what I wanted."

"Unless it's like Lulu said," Cherry pointed out. "He could have been acting threatening and things escalated and you were either defending yourself or it was an accident and you freaked out."

"Neither of those things happened," said John firmly. "I didn't kill him. But I'm glad he's dead." The hate fairly dripped from his words.

"Okay," said Cherry with a sigh. "You didn't kill him. Fine. Did you see or hear anything during your reconnaissance mission that could help us out? Who do you think killed Reuben? Because somebody did."

"I don't know. And I really don't care. He's dead and my house is in limbo and now I'm going to have to figure out how to pull money together to finish the construction. But that Brody? I wouldn't trust him. I'm sure y'all are convinced I'm the bad guy in all of this, but you should be considering someone like him," said John.

"Why is that?" asked Lulu.

"When I was hanging outside his booth, I was listening to hear whether Reuben was in there or not. He clearly wasn't, because Brody and his wife were talking very freely. They were talking about a partnership that Brody and Reuben were in—a partnership that was a total disaster. It didn't even sound like a real partnership—it sounded to me like Brody just lent Reuben money. And Sharon was furious, believe me. She said that if Reuben needed money so bad, he should be working for it. That he spent all day lounging around in his underwear and drinking. She wasn't real happy about their money being wasted . . . about as happy as I was about mine going down the drain."

John took a deep breath, gave them both a tight smile, and said, "Look, it's been great talking to you." His tone was sarcastic. "Good luck finding out who killed Reuben. I've got to go to work. Maybe if I work hard, in a couple of years I might be able to start rebuilding the inside of my house."

In a few seconds, he was gone.

Chapter

9

Cherry and Lulu walked back to Lulu's car and sat there a minute with the motor turned off. "Now what?" asked Cherry finally. "That somehow didn't turn out the way I thought it might. If we'd surprise him by confronting him with his motive and the fact he was being sneaky, and then he'd confess right there in his driveway. We'd call Pink over and everything would be hunky-dory and Lulu and Cherry would have saved the day again."

Lulu glanced at her watch. "Why don't we head over to Aunt Pat's? We can hang out on the porch with lemonades and talk about it before the lunch crowd comes in. I feel like I need to digest what John was telling us. And it wouldn't hurt to have some blueberry muffins to digest along with it."

Thirty minutes later, they were doing exactly that. Everything always seemed a little brighter with blueberry muffins and lemonade.

"We might have been naïve," said Lulu thoughtfully, putting down her empty plate. "Did we really think that John was going to blurt out a full confession to us because we startled him? We don't even know if the man was involved."

Cherry blew out a sigh. "They always confess in the movies and on TV."

"If they *did* it. And sometimes not even then." Lulu stopped talking when her cell phone started going off with a "Zip-a-Dee-Doo-Dah" ringtone. "Ack! Where is it? Where is it?" She frantically glanced around her.

"Here!" said Cherry, grabbing up Lulu's large, colorful pocketbook and shoving it at her, staring at her with wide eyes as if she'd thrown a bomb on Lulu's lap.

Lulu went tearing through the bag, pushing aside a fat wallet, drugstore cosmetics, and an extra pair of hose and finally finding the phone. "Hello?" she asked anxiously. She felt herself relax as she heard Sharon's voice. She mouthed "Sharon" at Cherry, who nodded and also slumped in relief at the lack of emergency.

"What's that?" asked Lulu, trying to hear Sharon's quiet voice on the phone. "What? If you're out driving around, why not come over to the restaurant? You know where it is, don't you? That way I can really hear what you're saying. Okay, I'll see you in a few minutes, then."

She set down the phone on the little table between Cherry and herself. "Hard to hear in that thing." Sometimes she worried that she was losing her hearing just the teensiest bit.

"I got swept away in your panic there, Lulu!" said Cherry, tilting back in the rocker as if she was flat worn out.

"I know. I'm sorry," said Lulu penitently. "I can't stand those cell phones. They startle me to death. Nobody ever calls me on them and I forget I have one. Half the time I don't remember to even turn it on."

Lulu's son came out on the porch in time to hear that last bit. Ben frowned at her, which had the effect of making him look like an irritated Captain Kangaroo. "That's exactly what I was talking about when I was fussing at you last week. I tried to call your phone and it was off. Sometimes I would actually like to be able to reach you. It might not be an emergency, it might be that I need to talk to you about something to do with the restaurant. Or that I need a ride over here. Or whatever. But if your phone's off . . ." He shook his head.

Lulu sighed. "I'm sorry, sweetie. You know I forget. And really, I only carry the phone for emergencies."

Ben said, "But emergencies go both ways, Mother. You're thinking that you want the phone when *you* have an emergency and you need to call *us*. But what if *we* have an emergency and need to call *you* and your phone is off? It's a two-way street."

Lulu thumped the palm of her hand on the arm of her rocker. "You are so right, Ben! I've been pretty selfish and I didn't even know I was. I'll start keeping the thing turned on. I'm turning over a new leaf."

Ben nodded and continued walking out of the restaurant. "You just do that, Mother. And remember to charge it at night."

Once Ben left, Cherry said, "Okay, now that that's all settled, tell me about the phone call. I'm kind of surprised that Sharon would call you. Actually, I'm surprised that you even knew your cell phone number well enough to give it to Sharon."

Lulu laughed. "I didn't. She asked for it, so I called her cell phone from mine so she could add my phone number to her contact list."

"I guess Brody meant what he said about Sharon really needing friends and not knowing anyone in Memphis yet," said Cherry.

"I guess so. She was real funny when I was leaving the festival for the last time. That's when she asked for my number so she could talk to me again. I'm thinking she thought she might miss the friendship and the connection that we all share and wanted a way to reach out to us," said Lulu.

Cherry said, "She's coming over now?"

She was. In another fifteen minutes, Sharon was walking in through the door and surprised both Cherry and Lulu with hugs.

Sharon didn't wear any makeup and her face was splotchy as if she'd been crying. Her pink nail polish was halfway picked off. Her black slacks and blouse were good quality, but didn't seem new. Lulu had noticed that the clothes Sharon usually wore always looked like they had designer labels—from a few years back. Like she'd had more money to shop with at one point, but now wasn't buying anything new.

"What's wrong, Sharon?" asked Lulu after Sharon had sat down in a rocking chair. "You sounded upset on the phone."

"This is going to sound so silly," said Sharon. But her eyes were worried. "We got a phone call from Reuben's lawyer and I learned that Brody and I were executors of Reuben's estate. And after all the stress of the last few days, for some reason, that bit of information made me fall apart."

Lulu nodded sympathetically. "The straw that broke the camel's back. I guess, though, that choosing Brody would have been natural—they've known each other for so many years."

Cherry said, "I'm surprised that Reuben went to the trouble to even get a will done. That's something that organized and responsible people do, and Reuben didn't sound so organized and responsible."

Sharon took a few gulps of lemonade from her glass, then put it down on the table. She gazed wearily at Lulu and Cherry. "It does seem kind of out of character, doesn't it? But apparently, Reuben had the will drawn up right after his divorce was final."

"He was probably in that legal mind-set at the time then," said Lulu. "He was in a courtroom so much he decided to go ahead and knock out his legal to-do list. Does that happen to y'all? It's funny—I'll have something like an ordinary doctor's appointment and it reminds me to knock out all my other health stuff. Then for the next couple of weeks, I'll be at the dentist and the eye doctor, and whomever else."

Sharon said, "I know what you mean. That's probably what happened."

"Maybe he was feeling real spiteful, too, and wanted to make sure his ex didn't get any of his money," said Cherry.

"Did he even have any money?" asked Lulu. "I was under the impression that he was squandering money that he had." Or borrowing money from Brody.

Sharon sighed. "Well, he did and he didn't. Lately, he wasn't working and pulling in an income and he was drinking his savings up. But there was money that he knew he was going to be getting, although he hadn't gotten it yet."

Lulu knit her brows. "What—an inheritance or something?"

"That's right. Reuben only had one living relative . . . his was a hard-living family with a habit of dying young. But he had an uncle who had done real well for himself and always doted on Reuben. He liked to brag about this rich uncle he had and how he was going to have tons of money one day." Sharon made a face. "Sometimes I wonder what Brody saw in Reuben, especially when I tell stories like this. But Reuben wasn't always like that. He was worse when he drank . . . that's why he was so awful lately. Because he didn't *stop* drinking."

Lulu said, "So this uncle—he ended up passing away?"

"Apparently so," Sharon said. "I think he died just a week or so before Reuben in a weird coincidence. Reuben ended up getting his estate. This uncle left all the money to Reuben."

Cherry said, "And Reuben did change his will. So who ended up being the beneficiary of Reuben's new will?"

Sharon sighed. "His son got a large sum of money, so I guess he was trying to look out for Finn, no matter what his ex was saying. But he also left a ton of money to Brody and me."

Cherry and Lulu stared at Sharon. "Really?" said Lulu finally.

"Well, he and Brody were good friends. And I guess he was really trying to stick it to his wife and make a point. And like I said, Reuben didn't have any other living family. Besides, Reuben didn't think he was going to die anytime soon, after all. But yeah—a bunch of money to us," said Sharon with a shrug.

Cherry and Lulu quietly digested this for a moment.

Then Cherry said, "So what are you so upset about? Sounds like this should have been good news."

Sharon groaned and put her hands to the sides of her forehead and rubbed like it hurt. The deep grooves at the corners of her mouth emphasized her unhappiness. "It's so complicated. We shouldn't be getting that money. Maybe we should get the money back that Brody lent Reuben to help him get by. Dawn is going to be furious— she's really going to go berserk. And the lawyer said that he knew some of Reuben's contracting customers were trying to sue Reuben and get their money back from unfinished projects and all. Apparently, he even had subcontractors that were demanding money from him. And then this John is seriously wanting money. Reuben's lawyer said that he was being especially pushy—almost threatening. So I don't really know what we should do."

"Do you think that settling all these claims will wipe out all the money?" asked Lulu.

"No, the lawyer didn't think so. Apparently, this uncle was really, *really* well off. But it's all such a headache," said Sharon. She continued absently picking off her nail polish.

Lulu said, "What do you think you're going to do? What seems like the best thing to do?"

Sharon said, "That's one of the reasons I'm visiting with y'all now. I'm trying to brainstorm. What I think is the best thing to do, and what I'm trying to convince

Brody that we should do, is to try to settle things with John. Like, right now. The madder he gets, the worse it's going to be."

"He's plenty mad," said Cherry. "We actually went to see him at his house. He was practically foaming at the mouth, he's so mad about the way that construction job went. And he sure doesn't have much money. I'm surprised he could even pay a lawyer to sue."

Lulu said, "That's probably why he'll be glad to settle. Then he can drop the lawyer and doesn't have to have an expensive court date or anything like that."

Sharon said, "That's what I'm hoping. I want to talk to him and be reasonable and see if we can come up with something that will make him happy. Maybe get Reuben's lawyer to draw an agreement up for him to get money when the estate is settled. I don't know John's last name or where he lives, though, and the last thing I want to do right now is to talk to that lawyer again. It takes forever for him to return phone calls anyway. Since y'all have been to his house, can you tell me where he lives?" She rummaged in her worn leather purse for a small notebook and a pencil.

Lulu dug in her pocketbook for the slip of paper with the address on it and handed it to Sharon. "I'm afraid we don't know a whole lot about John. He seems to be single, doesn't have a whole lot of money, and is mighty angry about the state his house is in right now."

Cherry nodded. "That's it, in a nutshell. He's a pretty

angry guy, Sharon. How are you going to approach him about this settlement?"

"I'm thinking I'll run by his house. I need to assess the damage anyway. You know—make sure he's not exaggerating what happened. Not that I think that he is," she hurried to say, "but it seems more businesslike to at least survey the damage."

"You should bring Brody with you then," said Lulu. She felt a chill run up her spine, but couldn't figure out why. "Don't go over there by yourself."

"Well, I know what you're saying, Lulu. But I haven't exactly convinced Brody that this is the right thing to do. I'm thinking this is something I should handle myself," said Sharon.

"We'll go with you!" said Lulu quickly. "Cherry and I would be happy to go to John's house with you."

"Pleased as punch!" said Cherry. "We even know the way and everything—it makes so much sense."

Sharon's eyes lit up with a grateful smile. "I really, really appreciate that, y'all. You don't know how much. But this is something I need to do by myself. John will be a lot more defensive if he sees a group of us coming at him. And if I have Brody with me, he's bound to feel even more so. No, I'm going to try to handle this myself. I'm sure that John will be perfectly reasonable."

John, however, was *not* perfectly reasonable. John was dead.

Pink came by Aunt Pat's the morning after Sharon's

visit while Lulu was putting out fresh tablecloths. Lulu raised her eyebrows when she saw him. "Working an odd shift, Pink? It's early for eating ribs. Well, not for me. But I'm up with the chickens." She broke off when she saw how grim Pink looked. "What's wrong? What's happened?"

"I'll tell you what happened, then you tell *me* what happened. There was a homicide that was discovered this morning by Sharon, your buddy in the next-door booth. It was John."

Lulu sat down in a booth. "Ohhh. Oh, how awful."

"But Lulu," said Pink, and she'd never heard such a stern voice from him, "I wasn't aware that a John even existed. And yet Sharon says she was talking to you and Cherry about him only yesterday on the front porch here."

Lulu felt herself color. "Mercy. You're right. I totally forgot about sharing that tidbit with you. Everything seemed to happen at once and I really haven't seen you much since the murder happened. I'm so sorry, Pink."

The apology seemed to smooth Pink's ruffled feathers. "Well, you know, it was kind of embarrassing to me. Made it look like I didn't know what was going on or all the connections in the case."

"You'd have ended up finding out about John," said Lulu. "You have to go through all the official channels, that's all. But someone would have pointed you in that direction—Reuben's lawyer, if nothing else."

Pink squinted at Lulu as if she were again talking about things she probably shouldn't know about.

Lulu said, "Pink, again, I'm awfully sorry about forgetting to tell you about John and his connection with Reuben. But—tell me. The murder."

"Sharon drove over to John's house this morning to try to talk to him before he left for work. She knocked and rang the doorbell, but there was no answer, so she tried the door handle," said Pink.

Lulu closed her eyes. "Why in heaven's name would she do that?"

"It was definitely not advisable. The door was unlocked, so she pushed it open and stuck her head in to call for John. But he was lying on the floor where she could see him. It appears he was hit with a heavy object from behind, then stabbed."

Lulu shook her head and sat quietly for a few moments. "Poor John." She looked up at Pink. "Sharon's not a suspect in John's death, is she? After all, why would she go out of her way to discover the body if she'd killed him? Seems like she'd want to let him lie there undiscovered for a while."

Pink sighed. "It's not that simple, Lulu. Think about it—it's the perfect setup. Sharon and her husband, Brody, know that this John is about to make a huge claim on their new inheritance. Sharon comes here to tell two witnesses that she plans to talk it out with John and reach a settlement. She makes it sound very levelheaded and reasonable. Then she or Brody goes over to John's house. He recognizes them and lets them in. They kill him. Then Sharon comes back later to 'discover' the body."

"I guess it's not as clear-cut as it seems," said Lulu. "She did seem so earnest, though."

"Naturally," said Pink. "She would have to, if she was planning an elaborate lie like that. Otherwise, you'd see right through her."

Lulu was starting to wonder how observant she actually was, though. And whether she was hopelessly naïve.

"I was talking to the neighbors," said Pink with studied casualness, "and asking them if they'd seen or heard anything unusual in the last couple of days."

Lulu swallowed. "Did they?"

"It's a remarkably unobservant group of neighbors," admitted Pink. "They didn't notice any visitors at John's house last night or any unusual cars. They didn't recognize pictures of Sharon or Brody. But they were able to give us an exact description of you and Cherry."

Lulu colored again. "Mercy," she said again. "I hadn't gotten around to telling you about all that." Pink didn't say anything and Lulu cleared her throat. "Would you like some corn muffins?"

Pink's grim demeanor broke into a grin. "Lulu, I'm not that mad. But you and Cherry are scaring me. What you did wasn't safe."

"We thought about our safety, actually," said Lulu quickly. "That's why we met John out in his driveway. Not like Sharon."

"Thankfully," said Pink. "What was it that you were trying to talk with him about?"

"We'd found out that he knew Reuben. And he'd carefully not mentioned anything about his connection to him before. We were miffed that he was lying to us and we wanted to hear more about this messed-up construction job that Reuben had been the contractor for," said Lulu.

Pink said, "And what did he say? How did he act?"

"He was real angry about the state his house was in. It was more of a quiet rage than someone going postal, though. He was definitely upset. But he claimed that he had nothing to do with the murder—that he was at the festival to try to dig up dirt on Reuben or to at least have a chance for him to talk to Reuben about the construction. Apparently, the situation had gotten to the point where Reuben was no longer returning John's calls or answering his door when he saw John outside," said Lulu.

They sat quietly for a moment, then Lulu said, "Can you tell me more about what you think happened to John? It's hard for me to believe he's dead when I saw him yesterday."

Pink said, "There's not too much more that we know right now. Because the door was unlocked, we think that John willingly let his killer in. So it was either someone that he knew, or someone that he recognized enough to let in. We think that it was probably last night, late but not too late. Possibly around ten o'clock. Whoever he let in didn't give him much of a chance to struggle. They probably came prepared and brought something with them that they could hit him with while he was leading them into another room."

"They brought something with them?" asked Lulu.

"It looks that way . . . we haven't found the murder weapon yet, so we're thinking the murderer took it away with them. It was probably something heavy but portable—like a hammer," said Pink.

Lulu winced. "And you said that he was stabbed, too?"

"Whoever did it wanted to make certain that John was dead. We think he was—that the blow from the heavy object killed him. But the killer wanted to make sure, so there was a butcher knife sticking out of his back. Again. Same as with Reuben."

Lulu said, "Could you tell anything from the knife?"

"Not really. It's a standard knife, available anywhere. It seems brand-new, so it was probably purchased for this very purpose," said Pink.

Lulu shivered.

"This murderer means serious business," said Pink. "And I want to make sure that you and Cherry aren't on his hit list. Watch your step—both of you."

Chapter
10

"So now we need to find out where Brody and Sharon live," said Cherry, heaving a sigh. They were both in Lulu's kitchen since Lulu had left for home right after Pink talked to her. "This is all so complicated. It would have been a lot easier if John had been guilty. He should have confessed to the crime and been trundled off to jail. Easy-peasy."

"His death sure does make things difficult," agreed Lulu. "I'll call Sharon real quick and get her address. And I'll bring food over in case she doesn't feel much like cooking today."

"Is that why your kitchen smells so good?" asked Cherry. "You must have been cooking up a storm."

"I ran by the store on the way home and I've been in

the kitchen for the last few hours. Sometimes cooking helps me relax—and I've definitely needed some relaxing lately. I cooked a ham and I've made a three-bean casserole and a pineapple casserole," said Lulu.

Cherry said, "It all sounds yummy—except for the three-bean casserole. I'm not usually wild about those. Too much vinegar."

"You might like this one then, since there's no vinegar at all in it. Just sour cream and cheese and a bunch of other yummy stuff. Vinegar is a little too tart for me, too. Except I do like my French fries dipped in vinegar," said Lulu.

Cherry made a face. "I'll pass on the French fries. But the casserole sounds like something I need the recipe for."

Sharon, who had sounded very un-Sharon-like on the phone, gave her address, and minutes later, Cherry and Lulu were at the house. It was, like John's, another subdivision and another ordinary suburban two-story house. Sharon answered the door. Her eyes were puffy and her face was blotchy. She still hadn't found the time to touch up her roots and the dark hair was starting to take over the blond hair. Lulu noticed that her nail polish was now completely picked off.

"Y'all must think that all I do is cry," she said. She noticed the bag that Lulu was carrying. "What's this?"

"Oh, I just thought you might not feel much like cooking," said Lulu. "So here's something you can have for supper tonight. Or it'll keep, if you'd rather have it another night."

Apparently, this small kindness was enough to make Sharon start crying again. Sharon looked like someone who was trying to hold it all together, but was failing miserably. Sometimes when you start crying, you can't ever seem to turn it off. Sharon scrubbed impatiently at her eyes. "Let's go in the kitchen," she said in a muffled voice.

Sharon led them toward the back of the house. They passed through a living room that still had a couple of boxes in one corner. The house had a lot of nice features—hardwood floors, granite countertops, and stainless steel appliances—but it didn't feel particularly homey. In fact, it didn't even seem like they'd personalized it at all, to make it their own. The exception was the kitchen, which was a cheerful room. "I love gingham in kitchens," said Lulu with a satisfied sigh as she saw the curtains and kitchen towels.

Sharon smiled at her as she put the barbeque into the refrigerator. "I do, too. That's as far as I've really gotten with the decorating. It looks like we just moved in last week instead of months ago. But between one thing and another, I haven't gotten around to it. And I've soured on home improvement projects in the last week," she said with a short laugh.

Cherry snorted. "I bet. This morning must have scared the living daylights out of you."

Lulu added, "But we know you might not want to re-live what happened, sweetie. We wanted to let you know that we were thinking of you and to see if there was any-thing we could do—run to the store for you, or something like that. When you've had a shock like you've had, it's hard to go back to doing regular, everyday errands."

"With a shock like this," said Sharon, "I actually want to talk about it. If I talk about it, maybe it won't seem as scary anymore or as real." She gave them a weak smile. "Next time I'll listen to y'all when you give me advice. I never should have gone to John's house to talk to him. Or I should have taken somebody with me, at least. I never thought it was going to end up like this."

"When did you go to John's house?" asked Lulu. "It must have been pretty early."

"It was," said Sharon. "I figured it would be easier to catch him when he was on his way to work."

This sounded familiar.

"But I wasn't sure if he had to be at work at eight or nine, so I showed up at seven thirty and waited. I painted my nails in the car, read a magazine, and still didn't see him. I knew he was short on money and I was surprised he wasn't heading out to work when it was past nine. That, of course, was when I should have given up and gone back home and tried to get Reuben's lawyer to talk to him or something. But instead, I went to John's door to see if I could get him to come out."

"I take it he didn't answer," said Cherry dryly.

"No, he sure didn't. I banged pretty hard on the door and rang the doorbell a few times and no one came. That was when I tried the door," said Sharon. "It was unlocked, so I walked in, calling his name. I knew right away that something was wrong. All the lights were on and it was a bright morning. Then I saw . . . him." She swallowed and tried to regain some control.

"That's *really* when I should have walked back out that door and dialed 911," she continued. "Thinking back on it now—well, I don't know where my head was."

"You were focused on what you were going to say to John when you saw him," said Lulu. "So . . . instead of leaving, you walked farther in?"

"I did. I don't think I really realized that John was dead . . . I was stunned. I wanted to get closer and see if I could help him. But when I got over to him, I saw that he was past needing help." Sharon took a deep breath.

Lulu was ready to jump in with some comforting words, but Sharon was determined to go on. "John's head was crushed on the back—I couldn't tell by what. And he was lying on his face. There was a knife in his back, too." She shivered.

Lulu reached out and gave Sharon a hug. "You must have been petrified! You went back out to your car then, didn't you?"

Cherry made a face. "I hope so. That would have been too creepy. I mean, I know none of us really knew John, but hanging out with a body?"

"That was finally what it took for me to come to my senses and go back to my car to call the police," said Sharon.

"Did they ask you a million questions?" said Cherry. "What kinds of things did they ask you about?"

Sharon said miserably, "I think they thought that I had something to do with it. Just from the questions they were asking me."

"Pooh!" said Lulu. "Why would they think a thing like that? You were there to try to patch things up with John and give him money."

"The police gave me the impression that they thought I might be making that part up," said Sharon. "They pointed out that it would be very convenient for John to be gone because Brody and I would end up with more money."

Brody walked in the kitchen. He looked like he'd had a full day and it was still early. His tone was belligerent. "That's true, but there were other people who stood to gain, too. I don't know why the cops are so focused on us. What about Reuben's ex-wife? She wasn't able to get any money out of him when he was alive, so why wouldn't she try to see what she could get out of him when he was dead?"

Cherry frowned. "Yeah, but I thought that he'd changed his will—"

"Sure," interrupted Brody, "but would Dawn know that? Somehow I don't think she knew that Reuben had been that organized. As far as she knew, Reuben either had an old will that named her as the beneficiary, or else it would go through probate court and either she or Finn would end up with *something*. And if Finn got some money, she'd likely be in control of it."

They all thought this over for a minute. Then Sharon added, "Maybe it's not even the money that would motivate Dawn. Maybe she was ready to take revenge on Reuben. He'd made her life pretty miserable lately, after all. She's clearly been unhappy since the divorce, too—she's gained a lot of weight and has all these health problems now."

"Taking revenge on Reuben would be one way of relieving frustration, I guess," said Cherry.

Lulu said, "I was wondering if y'all knew someone who works for me at the restaurant. It seems that he's connected somehow to Reuben. Or that he was." Lulu described the waiter, Tim, to Brody and Sharon.

Brody seemed to instantly know whom they were talking about. "Oh, sure. He used to be a friend of Reuben's. Reuben would share pictures online that showed them at different stuff together. Their wives were friends first—maybe they worked together. Then Reuben and him got to be buddies. I think he was Reuben's best friend . . . locally anyway. I was real close to Reuben, but I didn't live in Memphis most of the time that I knew him."

"Do you think that he could have had something to do with Reuben's death?" asked Sharon. She sounded hopeful, but who could blame her, considering that she was a suspect herself.

Cherry said, "But why would he be? That's what I don't understand. Why would a friend of his be considered a suspect? It's not like he was in the will or anything, right?"

"Were they still friends?" asked Lulu. "Were Reuben and Tim still going out and doing things together?"

Brody said, "Since I've moved to Memphis, I've not seen Tim around Reuben at all. Not a single time."

"So, what's the next step, Sherlock?" asked Cherry as they finally got back in the car.

Lulu sighed. "As much as I hate to say it, I need to be talking to Tim. I don't know what the connection between Tim and Reuben was, but there had to be one. Whatever their relationship was, it apparently went sour. I'd sure like to know why."

"You're going back to Aunt Pat's then?" asked Cherry.

"I sure am. You want to hang out at the restaurant today? I'm planning on making some lemonade pie and you can share it with me," said Lulu.

"You know I'd love to . . . especially with that pie. I guess you'll have to share it with the twins or Derrick instead, though—I've got to spend time at my other hangout today," said Cherry with a grin.

"You're a docent at Graceland today?" asked Lulu. "I tell you, I've slap lost track of the days lately."

"Murder has a way of making that happen," said

Cherry breezily. "But yes, it's my day to docent and you know I wouldn't miss it. I never can get enough of Graceland."

"Are you going dressed up in your Rock and Ribs Elvis costume?" asked Lulu innocently.

"No way!" said Cherry, shaking her head vehemently. "Between those shoes and that wig, I was hot and tired at all times. Nope, I'm wearing my old lady shoes with the comfy insoles and my hair pulled back in a ponytail. Comfort all the way!"

Lulu dropped Cherry off at her house and then headed to Aunt Pat's. The lunchtime crowd was dying down and it was nearly time for the kids to arrive from school. She spotted Tim, who dropped his gaze as soon as he saw her glancing his way.

Lulu walked over to him and said in a quiet voice, "Tim? I wanted to talk to you for a while. Is now a good time?"

Tim's pale face got even whiter, making a stark contrast to his too-dark hair. "Now? No, not right now. I've still got a couple of tables I'm waiting on."

"Okay," said Lulu. "What's your schedule like today? Will you still be here for the supper shift?"

Tim nodded, still avoiding Lulu's gaze.

Lulu repressed a sigh. The last thing she wanted to do was scare Tim off before she could even talk to him. "All right, so you'll be here for a while, then. If you don't mind, could you come and find me after your tables leave? I'm going to be on the front porch . . . and we can talk in the office when you're ready."

Tim nodded again, mumbled something about needing to get an order to a table, and hurried off.

Lulu watched him go. Was he shy? Tired? Anxious? Or did he have something to hide?

True to her word, she grabbed a pitcher of sweet tea and headed to the front porch. Her feet were hurting her just the slightest bit, and she thought back on how much she'd been standing up lately. Especially at the festival. She must have walked for miles to get to the Graces' booth and back—and then there were the times she walked the twins around, too.

As soon as she plopped down in a rocking chair and poured herself a glass of tea, she saw Morty coming onto the porch. "Oh good!" she said, smiling at him. "I was hoping a friend could come by and talk with me. I need to be distracted. My feet are bothering me today."

Morty said, "Welcome to the club. I must have ruined mine from years with the blues band." He settled down in the rocker next to hers and stretched out his legs with a sigh. They both rocked quietly for a minute, enjoying the sound of the ceiling fan and the murmur of voices from Beale Street.

Morty said, "Anything new?"

Lulu gave a short laugh. "That's right—you wouldn't know. Oh, mercy, Morty. It's been such a day." She filled him in on what had happened to John.

Morty gave a low whistle. "This sure sounds like trouble, Lulu. Don't you think you better back off? Seems like whoever the murderer is might be going after people who know too much."

"That might be. After all, John had hinted that we should be investigating elsewhere," said Lulu. "Maybe he was murdered because of what he knew."

"Somebody is desperate, I'll bet," said Morty. "That's when all kinds of bad things start happening. They've got to be bound and determined to keep anybody from knowing what they've done."

Lulu looked behind her and said in a soft voice, "You spend a lot of time here, Morty. What's your opinion of our waiter, Tim?"

"He's a good guy," said Morty with a nod. "Always remembers my name. He even knows what I usually order. And I've seen him play with the twins before— that's not in his job description, but it's only because he's being nice. Why? Are y'all having problems with him?"

Lulu shook her head. "Not really. But he somehow might be connected to some of what's going on."

Morty said, "I did notice one thing recently, though. He was on the phone here at the restaurant—the one in the break room, you know. I was on my way past the break room to the restroom and I happened to see him. He was real anxious. In fact, I thought he was fixing to cry."

"When was that, Morty? Can you recollect?" asked Lulu.

"I want to say that it was a couple of weeks ago," said Morty. "I don't have any clue who he was talking to, of course. In fact, when I saw how upset he was, I wanted to hurry past as fast as I could so that he wouldn't think I was trying to be nosy."

Could Tim have been talking to Reuben then? What was the problem between the two men?

Morty glanced at his watch. "Isn't it about time for Derrick to come back from school? Today was the day he was bringing his new friend, Finn, with him for me to show him tips for playing the trumpet."

"Was that today? I'm so messed up with time lately. Yes, he should be in any minute—" She broke off as they heard voices approaching the restaurant. "That's likely him now."

A moment later, Derrick came onto the porch with Finn. Finn smiled at them, but shifted from one foot to the other as if he felt uncomfortable. It must have been catching, because Derrick suddenly seemed uncomfortable, too. Discomfort was definitely a teenage affliction, but Lulu knew a pretty good cure. "Y'all want some bread pudding? I made some last night."

Their hopeful faces gave her the answer and she scooted off to the kitchen to warm the pudding and serve it with vanilla ice cream. When she got back, Morty was making small talk with Finn as if the boy were an accomplished professional musician and they were swapping trade secrets. And Finn was eating it up as fast as he ate up the bread pudding. Morty was holding his trumpet like an old friend and playing it intermittently while Finn tried mimicking him. This went on for nearly an hour until Morty started looking worn out—still happy, though. Lulu could tell that he thrived on sharing his love of music with an aspiring musician.

She was about to gently interrupt and redirect Finn when Derrick said casually, "Granny Lulu, you seem like you need to put your feet up for a while. Have you had a long day?"

The question had the effect of stopping her in her tracks. She hadn't planned on mentioning the murder to the boys, but the innocent inquiry threw her off track. Her eyes widened helplessly at Morty.

Morty was apparently not in the mood to tread lightly. "There was a man named John who was at the festival and hung out in the Graces' booth some. Unfortunately, he just died."

Derrick's brows knit. "Just died? What happened to him?"

"Well, he was murdered," said Morty. "And Sharon from the tent next to the Graces? She discovered him."

Derrick said something along the lines of what a crazy couple of weeks it had been . . . but Lulu's eyes were on Finn. His face was white and his fingers gripped the arms of the rocking chair he was sitting in.

While Derrick asked Morty more questions, Lulu leaned over to speak quietly to Finn. "You okay? Did you know John?"

He quickly shook his head, looking away. "I didn't really know him, but I did know who he was. I'd seen him around at the festival, that's all."

Lulu could swear for some reason that she saw anger in Finn's eyes.

Chapter

11

Morty noticed the stress on the young musician's face and said, "Okay! Let's get back to the music, Finn. Want to play a few more minutes? Then I'm probably going to have to take a break until next time."

Finn's face lit up at the mention of a next time. "Sure. I was sounding better, wasn't I?"

"I'll say. If you want to try this again after school later this week, I'm game."

Finn tried to act nonchalant, but couldn't pull it off. "Okay. That'd be great!"

Sara stuck her head out the door from the dining room. "Lulu, I hate to bother you, but could you step in and help me wait on the tables for a while?"

"Of course." Lulu stood up and smiled at Morty and the boys. "Y'all have fun out here." She followed Sara inside. "We're low on help this afternoon?"

"Well—we *weren't*. It's a funny thing. One of our waiters apparently left before his shift was over."

Lulu stopped walking and Sara turned to face her. "Which waiter?"

"Tim."

By suppertime, they'd gotten another waiter to fill in for them. Lulu was actually relieved to leave the restaurant—an unusual thing. But when your feet were already hurting, waiting tables wasn't exactly the best thing for them.

Back home, Lulu breathed a sigh of relief. Her little home was almost as comforting to her as the restaurant . . . and today, it was even more so. The rooms were cozy with dark hardwoods and old wooden furniture, cheerful scatter rugs, and puffy white curtains. Tonight, though, it was her oversized sofa that was the coziest. She'd managed to grab a bite to eat in between tables at the restaurant, so now all she wanted to do was lie back on the sofa. She wasn't usually too much of a TV person, but tonight she had this urge to find the most mindless show on the air and watch it until she fell asleep. Which, the way she was feeling right now, wouldn't take very long.

Lulu took off her lace-up shoes, stretched out on the sofa, pulled a crocheted blue-and-white blanket over her legs, and fumbled with the remote as she looked for a likely candidate for mindless viewing. Just her luck— every single one of the shows was mindless tonight. She settled for a reality show where the participants all seemed to be competing for the opportunity to travel around the world for a year. She felt her eyelids growing heavy.

Lulu jumped at a noise. Was that a knock on her door? Or had she dreamed it in her half-awake state? She lay there, frozen, eyes wide, waiting to see if there was another one.

There was.

Lulu raised herself up on the sofa and stared at the door. Who on earth would be out knocking at her door— it was after nine o'clock. She didn't have the kind of neighbors who would come by asking for eggs or giving her peaches at that time of night. She stood up and walked quickly over to the back door and peered out the side window next to the door. There was a thin curtain over the window, but she could still see through it— when the light was on, that is. Now all she could see was the outline of a man.

She flipped on the porch light and peered through the curtain again. It was Tim. He had his hands shoved down in his pockets and was staring at the window. "Tim?" she hollered, since the door was pretty thick. "That you?"

"Yes ma'am," came Tim's serious voice. "It sure is."

"Isn't it kind of late to come calling? What happened

to you earlier tonight? You and I were going to talk at the restaurant." Lulu felt uneasy about this unexpected visit in the light of recent events.

"Yes ma'am, it is kind of late and I'm sorry about that. I'm sorry about cutting out of Aunt Pat's earlier, too. I'm sorry about a lot of stuff, actually." And with that, Lulu's jaw dropped open as the man burst into tears right there on her front porch.

That was all it took for Lulu to unlock the door and open it. She took Tim by the arm and propelled him into her kitchen. If he was sobbing that hard, he wasn't likely to be sticking a knife into her at the same time. "It's all right, Tim, everything is just fine."

He shook his head that he didn't have any murderous intent and Lulu bustled around her kitchen, putting together the hearty type of sustenance that she imagined a man suffering real distress might want.

And she had no doubt that Tim was in serious distress.

When he'd finally settled down enough to be able to talk, he took a deep breath and said, "I wanted to tell you why I ran off today and how I know Reuben Shaw. Because I did know him—he and I used to be friends."

He stopped there and thought about that for a moment. Lulu said, "Reuben used to be a good friend to a lot of different people, didn't he? I've heard others talk about their friendships with him."

Tim looked down at his plate, now completely clean of all peach cobbler. When Lulu made to give him more, he stopped her with a small smile. "I'm all right, thanks. Yes, we were pretty good friends, and Reuben seemed like a nice enough guy. Our wives worked together at a preschool and they had gotten to know each other well enough at work that they started going out to movies and shopping together on weekends. Eventually, they decided it would be good for all of us to get to know each other."

"So the husbands started hanging out, too?" asked Lulu. "What kinds of stuff did y'all do?"

"Mostly things around the house at first. Like cookouts. Reuben was high on his barbequing skill," said Tim with a laugh.

Lulu said ruefully, "Yes, I encountered his bravado at the festival."

"To be truthful, he was a good cook. Not in your league, of course, Mrs. Taylor. But real good. So we did that kind of thing at first—go to cookouts and our kids' Little League games—stuff like that. But then things changed. I don't know if Reuben started getting bored, or what. He wanted to go out more—like to clubs and bars and those kinds of places. He was one of those people who probably had a bit of a wild streak in him, and he'd been keeping it pushed down for a lot of years. I guess it was time for it to come back up to the surface," said Tim.

Lulu said, "So y'all started going out at night and drinking together? Without your wives, I'm guessing."

"That's right. It wasn't like we were doing any more

than drinking, though—we weren't meeting women or anything like that. We'd go out and drink and talk for a while, then we'd come home. Although sometimes Reuben could be a real flirt, but I never saw him take things any farther than that," said Tim.

"What was Reuben like when he drank?" asked Lulu.

Tim said, "At first, he was okay. He was louder than usual. But it wasn't like he was mean or like it changed his personality at all. At first."

Lulu waited. She figured they'd come to the point in the story where she'd find out what changed Reuben into the person that his longtime college friend didn't even recognize anymore. And what had changed a man who was supposed to be a talented contractor into someone who never even showed up for work anymore.

"One night, Reuben and I went out. It's been almost two years ago now. Reuben had more to drink than he usually did. It seemed like every time we went out together, he'd drink more each time. This time he drank a couple more drinks than usual. I should have said something," said Tim. "I should have stopped him before he got to that point."

Tim's face was somber and Lulu could tell that this was a conclusion he'd reached a long while ago—that he should have stepped in. He wasn't asking her for her opinion.

"Unfortunately, he was also the one who was driving. I'd had plenty to drink myself, so I wasn't exactly wanting to take the car keys. But I should never have let Reuben drive back home," said Tim, gazing at Lulu with hollow eyes.

Lulu said, "Tim, you know that it's always easier to make the right decision when you're looking back."

He nodded. "But I ignored that voice inside me that night, telling me that I needed to call a cab. Or call Dawn, or my wife. Instead, I let Reuben swagger off to the car. Sometimes he could be pigheaded and this was one of those times. He obviously thought he was fine and was bragging that he was somebody who could hold his liquor."

Tim put his head in his hands like he needed to support himself to get through the next part of his story. "Reuben had the windows down and the radio blaring real loud and he was in real high spirits. He drove fast. It was late—probably after eleven, and the streets were dark . . . we were driving on smaller roads that didn't have streetlights."

Tim took a deep breath and stared at Lulu's kitchen ceiling like he could see what had happened that night up there. "Reuben looked down and fiddled with the radio to change the stations. He pulled the steering wheel over to the side when he did—and ran right into a pedestrian on the sidewalk."

"On the *sidewalk*?"

"Yes, he was that far off the road." Tim sighed. "We stopped the car, but not for long. We got out long enough to see that the man was lying completely still—and that Reuben's car had knocked him clear off the sidewalk and into a tree. Then Reuben told me to come on, he jumped into his car, revved his motor, and got out of there as fast as he could."

Lulu said slowly, "Did you try to get Reuben to stop? To stay with the man?"

Tim's voice cracked as he said, "No. To my complete and utter shame, I didn't try to make him stay and see if we could have helped that man. In fact, I pushed Reuben to get us out of there. All I could think about was my own life—my wife, my children, my job. I felt like an accomplice and I guess when I urged him to get out of there, I was acting like an accomplice. I didn't stop to try to get medical attention for someone who might have been dying in front of me. I was totally weak. I hate myself every single day for it."

"What happened when you got back home?" asked Lulu. "I bet that's when it all started to sink in."

Tim nodded. "It started sinking in then and it hasn't stopped from that point on. I live with the guilt from that night every day. When Reuben pulled up in my driveway, we both sat there and stared at my house without saying a word. I don't know how long we stayed like that. I was half listening for police sirens—figuring that they were on their way to pick us up. It felt unbelievable that we were going to get away with having done something like that."

"Did Reuben say anything? While y'all were sitting there?" asked Lulu.

Tim gave a hoarse laugh. "He said, 'What just happened? It never happened.' That was it. And for him, it was something he wasn't going to acknowledge or claim from that point on."

"So he's never talked about it with you?" asked Lulu. "You never even came up with a plan for what to do if someone ever found out? Or if the police got a tip and showed up on your doorsteps?"

"No. And it was the last time that I ever went out with him or visited his house," said Tim. "Our wives figured we'd had some kind of argument."

Tim stared blankly across Lulu's kitchen. "It almost felt like a nightmare. When I woke up the next morning, I wondered if I'd dreamed the whole thing. I *hoped* I'd dreamed the whole thing," he added in a fervent voice. "But then, when I got on the computer the next morning, the story was on the local news. A fatal hit-and-run."

"So the pedestrian did die," said Lulu sadly.

"Yes. But Reuben and I didn't even wait to see if we could help him. Maybe it wasn't an instant fatality. Maybe he'd still be alive," said Tim.

He blew out a long sigh. "And that's when my life started falling apart."

Lulu waited for him to continue, but he was having a hard time talking—as if the words hurt even saying them.

"I couldn't deal with what had happened and with my

part in it. I got to be obsessed with the news story—and there wasn't even that much information on it. They never really had a lead. The news stations put pictures of the man's family up—cute kids, pretty wife. Showed a picture of them at the man's funeral. His name was Kyle." Tim looked up at Lulu, his eyes full of tears. "It's all so pointless."

"You didn't tell your wife what had happened?" asked Lulu.

"I was too ashamed of myself," said Tim. "I almost didn't even want to admit to myself that I'd been part of such a horrible event. So I spent most of my time hiding from it. I felt like I was turning into Reuben. I started drinking more and more. My wife and I kept fighting with each other. She finally ended up taking the kids and leaving." Tim rubbed his temples.

"Is that what happened to Reuben, too?" asked Lulu. "I know he's divorced now and you'd said he was still married two years ago."

"Like I mentioned, I hadn't been back in touch with Reuben since that night. But I guess it must have been what happened." Tim shrugged. "It didn't stop there, either. At least, it didn't for me. Because I was drinking so much, trying to forget what happened, I couldn't hold down a job. Every place I worked, I kept getting fired. I either wouldn't show up, or I'd show up to work drunk. It even got to the point where I couldn't pay my rent. So then I didn't even have a place to live anymore."

Lulu said, "The same thing must have happened to Reuben. I kept hearing that his contractor business had really fallen apart. He apparently wasn't showing up to work, or placing orders for building supplies, or doing any of the things he was supposed to do. His business, which people had really praised, went downhill real fast."

Tim said, "Probably. I did hear that his business was starting to get a bad reputation that it hadn't had before."

"Something must have changed for the better for you, Tim," said Lulu. "I've never seen you drunk on the job. And today was the only time when you weren't at work when I was expecting you to be."

"What happened was me realizing that the only thing that was going to help make this mess better was to own up to what I'd done and to try to pay my debt in a small way. Maybe it would end up being more healing for the victim's family, too—to at least know what happened that night. Give them closure," said Tim.

Lulu nodded. "You decided to tell the police. But you wanted to tell them the whole story—and that meant getting Reuben involved."

Tim hung his head. "I thought I should tell Reuben my plans. I'd heard through the grapevine that things weren't going so well for him, either. I figured I could approach him real reasonably about it and he would go with me to the police station. Then we could pay the price for what we'd done and finally move on with our lives. The way I was going, living out of my car, not able to keep a job, drinking all day—I know I'd have been dead in a few years."

"What did Reuben say?" asked Lulu.

"Well, it was a real short phone conversation," said Tim. "I think the only reason he didn't hang up on me as soon as he heard my voice is because he was curious. He wanted to hear what I had to say. But as soon as he did hear what was on my mind, he hung right up," said Tim.

"He wasn't ready to own up to it," said Lulu.

"He sure wasn't. From what I could see, he had absolutely no intention of ever admitting what he'd done," said Tim.

"But he must have known that you could still go to the police and tell them what had happened that night, even if he didn't want to. You could still report it," said Lulu.

Tim said, "Yeah, but if I didn't have the actual driver of the car with me and admitting to it, then it was basically my word against his."

"What about the car? The one that he wouldn't let his wife drive anymore? I bet the police could get forensic evidence that it was involved in the hit-and-run," said Lulu.

Tim said, "But I wasn't even sure he still owned that car. It's been two years and he could have waited for the story to die down and then sold it to somebody."

"That's true. So you didn't give up with the one phone call obviously," said Lulu.

"No. I tried calling Reuben whenever I had a chance. I called him from your office a couple of times, Mrs. Taylor," said Tim in the attitude of somebody who wants to come clean on just about everything.

Lulu waved her hand in a dismissive gesture. "Oh, Tim, I don't care about that."

"And lately, I used the computer in the office to follow what's been going on in the news with Reuben's murder," said Tim. "I don't have a computer or anything at home. In fact, I've only now got an apartment." He seemed proud, though, at the accomplishment.

Lulu beamed at him. "Tim, that's wonderful. I'm pleased as punch that life is turning around for you."

"It is. But going back to right before Reuben's murder, I still wanted to own up to my part in what happened that night. So I didn't let up. I really think that Reuben thought that I was going to let it drop if he didn't agree to confess with me. Finally, I managed to call him from a pay phone and he picked up and listened for a few minutes. I told him that I was going to the police whether he planned on confessing or not," said Tim.

Lulu said, "I bet that didn't go over well with him."

"It sure didn't. That's when the tables were turned and he tried harassing *me*. Except that he didn't know where I lived since I wasn't living at the house where I used to live when he knew me. He apparently tried calling the numbers on his caller ID that he knew I'd used to call him—one time someone at the restaurant told me I had a call from some guy and I knew it must be him. I told them to tell Reuben that I was no longer working at Aunt Pat's."

"Then I came across Reuben at the festival—where I was volunteering and sometimes did an odd job for pay. He didn't even notice me at first," said Tim.

Or maybe he hadn't recognized him. Lulu bet that Tim had changed a lot since the days when he and Reuben were going out on the town together. The hard life he'd led really showed on him.

"Once he did see me, I could see that he was totally furious," said Tim. "All he wanted to do was to pressure me to keep from telling the police about what had happened. He was lucky that I'd had such a busy time at the restaurant lately with all the extra diners in town that I hadn't had an opportunity to get to the police station yet. One time I thought about telling Pink when he was eating there, but I didn't want to make him do work-related stuff while he was on a lunch break."

"What happened during your talk with Reuben?" asked Lulu.

"It was more than a talk," said Tim ruefully. "He pulled me off to the side so we could argue in private. He told me that if I went to the police, he would tell them that *I* had been the one driving his car home that night.

That I'd thought he had too much to drink and took his car keys and drove us back in his car. That *I'd* been the one to run over that guy."

Lulu sighed. "And it would be your word against his, of course."

"That's right. I even talked to a guy I knew who was a lawyer. He said that I probably wouldn't even get charged with anything as a passenger—maybe I might get charged as an accessory or an accomplice . . . that had happened in other states before. But as the driver—we're talking about serious jail time."

"Obviously, that was the last time you saw Reuben," said Lulu.

"That's right," said Tim quietly. "And I know now the police will think I had a motive for killing him. But I didn't. All I want to do is to own up to my role in that night and maybe even make some kind of reparations to the victim's family. Maybe even do volunteer work to pay back the community in general. I want a clean slate. I think that's why I dodged out of Aunt Pat's earlier today, Mrs. Taylor—I hated to think that I might lose the regular job that I'd finally gotten. I know you'd somehow gotten wind of my involvement with Reuben."

"Where were you when Reuben was murdered?" asked Lulu.

"According to what I read on the computer from the news stories, I would have still been at the festival," said Tim in a quiet voice. "But why would I have killed him?"

he asked Lulu, as if trying to see what motive someone might come up with. "I was trying to turn my whole life around."

"Could it be that maybe Reuben got real aggressive with you? He'd already picked a fight at the festival and was extremely belligerent when I saw him. If you murdered him, it could have been self-defense," suggested Lulu.

Tim shook his head. "No. Much as I've wished that Reuben Shaw was never part of my life, I'd never be able to kill him. Not even in self-defense."

But he looked away from Lulu when he said it. Because he knew that he wouldn't be very trustworthy after what had happened the night of the hit-and-run? Or because he'd murdered Reuben and was lying about it?

"You didn't see or hear anything at the festival that night that could help us figure out who killed Reuben?" asked Lulu.

"Only one thing," said Tim. "I did see Reuben's old friend Brody there. I recognized him from all the pictures of Reuben and Brody hunting and fishing together."

"What was Brody doing when you saw him?"

"He was carrying a tarp and acting sneaky. Glancing around him to make sure no one was watching," said Tim. "And that's all that I saw at the festival."

"Did you hear the most recent news about the case?" asked Lulu.

Tim was anxious again. "No, I haven't had a chance

to get a newspaper or read the news on a computer yet. What's happened now?"

"John, who was an unhappy customer of Reuben's, has been murdered, too. It happened last night," said Lulu.

Tim's expression was bewildered. "What's going on? Why would somebody kill one of Reuben's customers?"

"We don't really know—but we're guessing that John knew something. He was hanging around our booths at the festival and might have seen or overheard something," said Lulu.

Tim shook his head. "Seems crazy to me. I didn't know this John—and I was at Aunt Pat's for a long shift last night. You can check in with the staff and see. I worked there until after we closed so that I could help clean up."

He searched Lulu's face, trying to see if she believed him. Lulu reached over and patted Tim's hand. "Thanks for all your help at the restaurant. You've done a great job. Don't worry about leaving before your shift ended tonight—I understand what you must have gone through lately."

Tim's face was relieved. "I'll stay past my shift tomorrow. And, Mrs. Taylor? Thank you."

Chapter

12

The next afternoon, Sharon came by Aunt Pat's. "Is it too late for me to get lunch?" she asked with a smile.

Minutes later, Sharon was tucking into a big plate of ribs, baked beans, and coleslaw. Lulu figured Sharon still needed a distraction, considering how upset she'd been the day before. So she talked to her about the restaurant. Lulu pointed out some of the old photos on the wall—family pictures that meant the most to her, as well as signed pictures of some of the famous diners who'd visited Aunt Pat's. She talked about how both she and her son, Ben, had grown up at the restaurant.

The stories seemed to both relax and interest Sharon, and she ate and asked a few questions, nodding from time to time. The quiet ended abruptly, though, with the appearance of Cherry. Her wildly colored red, orange, and gold dress reminded Lulu of a torrent of fall leaves.

"Aunt Pat's is the best place to hang out, isn't it?" she crowed. Cherry gave Lulu and Sharon one-armed hugs. "How's it going, Sharon?" asked Cherry more soberly. "Are things looking up at all?"

"I guess they haven't gotten any worse anyway," said Sharon dryly. "Considering I haven't discovered any more murder victims. And Reuben surprisingly had a decent lawyer—left over from his business days, I'm thinking. So he's been more of a pleasure to deal with than I'd have thought."

"I did have one thing to ask you about, Sharon," said Lulu. "Sometimes we have these little mysteries that pop up that need figuring out."

Sharon was already shifting uncomfortably as if she somehow knew what was coming.

"Someone spotted Brody at the festival before Reuben was murdered. He said that he saw Brody holding a tarp and glancing around him like he didn't want anybody seeing him," said Lulu.

Sharon turned bright red. "Ohhh. That. Yes." She took a sip of her tea, then took another long sip and cleared her throat. "Brody took your tarp," she finally said with a sigh, not able to meet Cherry's eyes.

Cherry's eyebrows shot up and her jaw dropped open. Lulu waited for Sharon to continue.

"I didn't want to say anything because I was embarrassed about it. I couldn't believe we were stooping so low for a dumb contest. You remember—it was starting to really rain a lot. And even though we'd put a lot of time into planning that booth and putting it up, we were short on tarps," said Sharon.

"And rain was probably starting blowing into your booth and getting your food wet," said Lulu, nodding.

"It was. Reuben had really been on us that day, too, trying to get Brody and me to feel all super competitive. Some of the time, we were rolling our eyes at each other, but some of the time it was sinking in, too," said Sharon.

"You were getting brainwashed," offered Cherry helpfully, now that she'd gotten over the fact that her new friend had helped steal something from her.

"We were, I guess. Brody had noticed that y'all had an extra tarp. Or two," said Sharon.

"We were set with the tarps," said Cherry, nodding complacently. "We might have had other problems . . . our booth might not have been as fancy as others and our ribs might not have been award-winning. But boy, we had tarps! It sure does rain in the spring here in Memphis."

"Maybe that was part of the problem," said Lulu. "Y'all didn't know how hard it rains here during the festival because you haven't lived in Memphis long."

Sharon gave them a grateful look, and hazarded a hesitant smile. "Thanks, Lulu. Or maybe we were being plumb stupid in lots of different ways. Stupid not to have thought of bringing more tarps. Stupid to have stolen y'all's when you'd been so careful to be prepared."

Lulu nodded and rocked in her rocker. "It happens to everybody sometimes."

"Anyway, the rain was pouring. Reuben had whipped us all up into a competitive frenzy and we weren't acting like we normally do. Our stuff was getting wet and Reuben would be back at the booth soon and he'd start yelling at us for not bringing enough tarps. All we needed was another argument that day," said Sharon with a rueful purse of her lips.

"He'd have jumped all over y'all's case that day," said Cherry, remembering. "He was definitely in the mood for a fight."

"When Brody was getting the tarp, he did notice something. He recognized Reuben's ex-wife, Dawn, leaving that narrow space between our two booths. She was hurrying away, and the rain was sheeting down, but he says he's sure it was her. She must have been spying on one of our booths—and we figured it probably wasn't the Graces' tent," said Sharon.

"Wonder what she was trying to find out?" asked Lulu, frowning over the new information.

"Well, either she was trying to find a good time to put some pressure on Reuben for child support or she was looking for the right time to kill him," said Sharon with a shrug. "I can't think of another reason why she'd have been there. Brody ended up telling the police about the tarp and about seeing Dawn. As you can imagine, his prints were all over that tarp. It wasn't like he ever thought that the police were going to fingerprint the thing—he thought he was simply swiping an extra tent that he'd put back later for y'all, when we were all packing up."

Cherry nodded. "So you think Dawn wanted to find an opportunity to squeeze more money out of Reuben?"

Sharon said, "Maybe. If you think about it, when else was she going to be able to see him? He wasn't doing his visits with Finn like he was supposed to. If she was going to try to put pressure on him at all, this was a good time to do it. The divorce changed her and made her really bitter. It sounded like she was real short on cash, too, and might have been trying to do anything to get Reuben to pay his child support and help her out."

"Except that maybe he didn't have a whole bunch of money left at the time," said Cherry. "Considering he hadn't been working steady and that he was drinking up most of what was in the bank."

"And his uncle hadn't passed away yet," said Lulu.

"Exactly. She wouldn't have really known how much money he had at the time—but she knew she wasn't getting any of it. We'd kind of followed what was going on by the way Reuben was complaining about her trying to get money out of him. Brody and I could tell that he wasn't treating her right. He acted like he resented giving her any money, at all. He was scornful about it all and said that Dawn was having health problems and expected him to help her out with Finn. Sneering about it," said Sharon.

"So will y'all forgive me for my involvement in the tarp episode?" asked Sharon, flushing again. "I've felt real bad about it since it happened. Especially after you've both been so nice to me."

"Don't think a thing of it," said Cherry. "That tarp didn't make a difference in the world to the Graces— we'd brought extra. Evelyn wanted to make extra sure that she didn't end up getting wet."

"Thanks," said Sharon, smiling at both of them. "And now that I've had a delicious lunch and relieved my conscience, I'd better head on out. I'm supposed to be meeting Brody at Reuben's lawyer's office."

After she left, Lulu sighed and said to Cherry. "Have you noticed that as we dig for information, no one ends up looking good?"

"I thought it was kind of mean of them to take our tarp, but it's all water under the bridge at this point," said Cherry with a shrug. "Although I wish Brody had just asked us. I'd have given it to him, even though his teammate was being a jerk."

"Sharon probably wasn't real happy with him at the time," said Lulu. "Reuben was a bad influence on a whole lot of people. I don't get the impression that John was that bad of a guy until Reuben got him all fired up about his house."

"Camping out in your own home would make you crazy after a while, for sure," said Cherry. "Can you imagine not having electricity or working plumbing? For a long time?"

"And Tim was a great guy," said Lulu thoughtfully, "Then Reuben messed him up." She glanced behind her real quick to make sure that he wasn't coming up behind her from the dining room.

"What's that?" asked Cherry, frowning.

"Let me fill you in on what happened after I went home last night," said Lulu.

After she'd told the story, Cherry gave a low whistle. "So Reuben even got his claws into Tim and screwed up his life, too. That's a champion bad influencer, for sure."

"Don't forget about Dawn, either," said Lulu. "From what I hear, she was a normal, fun-loving person who liked going out to dinner with the lady she worked with and was a good wife to Reuben and a good mother to Finn."

"And the next thing you know, she's all bitter and hiding outside booths trying to find the perfect moment to put pressure on Reuben," said Cherry. "Or murder him."

"Desperation is a funny thing," said Lulu. "And I'm pretty sure Dawn was a desperate woman."

Right then, there was noisy shuffling around on the steps leading up to the porch, so Lulu and Cherry shushed up. It was Dawn. She acted like her usual self, though—not overly friendly, but her normal somewhat grouchy self. But the way she didn't exactly meet Lulu's gaze made her wonder if maybe she hadn't overheard some of their conversation.

"I figured you'd probably be here," she said to Lulu. "I know how the restaurant business is—my dad used to be in it when I was a kid. He was always there."

Lulu smiled at her. "That's the way it always seems. I'm lucky, though, that this is basically where I grew up. It's a second home to me, so I don't feel bad about being here so much. Did you need to talk with me about something?"

Dawn hesitated, then plopped down next to Cherry in one of the wooden rocking chairs. "I was checking in on Finn, that's all. I've been wrapped up in my own worrying lately, and haven't been giving him the time that I should have been."

"Easy to do," said Lulu, nodding.

"When he told me that he was hanging out with Derrick, I thought maybe that was a good thing. Finn doesn't have a whole lot of friends—he's a quiet guy and keeps to himself," said Dawn. "I guess the divorce didn't help him become any more outgoing, either. At any rate, he got even more quiet after Reuben and I split up."

Lulu said, "Derrick seems happy to hang out with Finn. Maybe he can introduce him to some of the people he knows, too."

"I hope so," said Dawn. "Finn told me he was also spending time here at the restaurant in the afternoons after school. Meeting an elderly black man here about music lessons?" Dawn sounded very confused. "Honestly, he didn't do a great job explaining it all to me, and when I tried to ask questions because I didn't understand, he got frustrated with me and stomped off."

Cherry laughed. "He sure sounds like a normal teenager to me."

"Morty is an old friend of mine," said Lulu. "He's been a fixture around Aunt Pat's for many years. He and two other friends had a blues band that was mighty popular back in the day and they still have gigs now, even though they're in their eighties. He was visiting with us for a few minutes in our booth and he and Finn got to talking about playing the trumpet. Finn was so interested that Morty offered to give him some help with it . . . tips and that kind of stuff. Not what you'd call a lesson, I don't think, but just extra help."

"That's awful nice of him," said Dawn. "I haven't been able to afford lessons for Finn, and he's been dying to learn to play the trumpet. Somebody I know from work had a trumpet that their child didn't need anymore and they gave it to him. He's been trying to figure it out on his own by playing around with it and by watching videos on the Internet. It's not the same thing." She shifted uncomfortably. "Do you think I should offer to pay Morty? This sounds like something that's taking up a lot of his time."

"You know, I have a feeling that it's a pleasure for

Morty to show him the instrument. His whole life, singing and trumpet playing were his favorite things. And to have a young person interested in what you're saying and hanging on your every word of wisdom when it comes to the trumpet? That's pretty rewarding, too."

Dawn seemed relieved.

"And I don't know if this is a regular thing, but it sounded like they were going to try to meet up here at the restaurant after school at least once a week. Derrick hangs out on the porch with them and usually eats a whole bunch, from what I can gather," said Lulu.

"Again—sounds like a normal teenager to me," said Cherry, snickering.

"Okay," said Dawn with a deep sigh. She sounded relieved that she at least had one thing that she didn't have to worry about.

Lulu hated to have to disturb Dawn's unusually happy mood, but since the woman was already making motions like she might be picking her pocketbook back up and leaving, she figured she didn't really have a choice. "Ah, Dawn. Could I get you a glass of iced tea or some food?"

"Thanks much, but I don't have the time right now. I've got a doctor's appointment I've got to get to," said Dawn, leaning over to pick up her purse.

Lulu said in a rush, "I guess you've heard about John. John, one of Reuben's customers?"

Dawn gave Lulu a blank stare.

"You mean the cops haven't asked you questions about

where you were when he was murdered?" asked Cherry in an incredulous voice. "They sure did ask me!"

Which might have been because neighbors had described Cherry and Lulu's outdoor conversation with John on the morning of the day he died. The police probably hadn't gotten around to talking to Dawn about his death, but that didn't mean that they wouldn't. Not that Lulu was going to tell Dawn that.

"Murdered? What? Who is John?" asked Dawn in a frustrated voice. "You said he was a customer of Reuben's?"

"Yes, and apparently a very dissatisfied one. Reuben hadn't finished his construction project and John paid him upfront, so he didn't have the money to pay someone else to complete it," said Lulu.

"I'm sure it made him fit to be tied, but that wouldn't have anything to do with me, would it? Sounds like that's something that's happened kind of recently. When Reuben and I were together, Reuben got up every day and went to work. Worked hard, too. That's one reason why it's totally annoying to me that he was sitting around in his bathrobe all day. The guy could pull in good money when he worked," said Dawn.

"Maybe John was somebody who Reuben would complain about to you when y'all talked to each other on the phone?" suggested Cherry.

"Are you kidding me? Reuben wasn't going to talk to me about *nothing*."

"Not even about visits with Finn?" asked Lulu quietly.

"Especially not visits with Finn. Everything Reuben was doing was to avoid any kind of financial responsibility. If he had visits with Finn, that would remind him that he had a child. If he dwelled too much on that, then maybe he'd think he should do something to support this kid. So no—we didn't talk. Not that I didn't call. I must've been hung up on dozens of times," said Dawn darkly.

"So you're saying you didn't happen to be over at John's house a couple of evenings ago," said Cherry.

Dawn put her hands on her hips. "I'm saying that I don't even know who this guy is! And no, if you need to have it spelled out, I didn't kill him. A couple of evenings ago, I was with Finn at home. Finn was trying to study for a big test and I helped him by calling out terms he was supposed to know. That's what I was doing. I'm a single mom—I don't have time to go out and murder people."

Cherry was opening her mouth to say something—probably something ill-advised—when Tim stuck his head out the door from the dining room into the porch. "Mrs. Taylor, I'm shifting out, but then I'm planning on coming back over here to help clean up before y'all close tonight. Was there anything else that you needed me to do before I left?" He smiled at Cherry, then glanced over at Dawn and appeared startled.

Dawn said slowly, "I didn't know you were working over here, Tim. How are you doing?"

180

Tim's face flushed. "I'm doing pretty well," he said in a quiet voice. But his fingers gripped the door tightly, Lulu noticed.

"It's fine if you want to clock out, Tim. Thanks for helping us out today," said Lulu.

He gave her a small smile and dodged back into the dining room.

Chapter

13

Dawn looked like the cat that had eaten the canary. "Of course, you know who Tim is, don't you? Your waiter? He used to be a friend of Reuben's—he was married to one of my coworkers at the preschool. And I don't know what happened between the two of them, but Reuben stopped speaking to Tim real abruptly and never spoke to him again. Not ever. I never did figure out why."

"Maybe," said Cherry sassily, "Tim figured out that Reuben was no good. Before you did, that is. Did you think that maybe Tim was the one who broke off that friendship and not Reuben?"

Apparently not, because a surprised expression flitted across Dawn's face.

"Like I said," growled Dawn, "I've got to get going to get to my doctor appointment. Thanks for watching after Finn," she said to Lulu. She glared at Cherry as she stomped off the porch.

Once the screen door had slammed shut behind her, Lulu puffed out a sigh. "Cherry, I don't believe Dawn is all that crazy about you."

"She doesn't know what she's missing," said Cherry, putting her stubby nose in the air. "I happen to be a fantastic friend. Even though I'm a friend who's dragging you into a murder investigation."

"Don't you think the police are focusing more on the other suspects?" asked Lulu. "After all, it's not like you even knew Reuben before the festival. And I can't think why you'd have wanted to kill John."

Cherry said gloomily, "It has to do with the fact that I had the opportunity both times. Maybe they think there's a connection between us that they haven't learned about yet. Who knows? Maybe they think that I killed Reuben in an angry, impulsive moment and then had to kill John because he knew about it."

"I guess they could think that," said Lulu. "But it sure seems unlikely."

"That's because you're my friend, Lulu."

"Pink is your friend, too!" said Lulu.

"But Pink isn't calling the shots. He's part of the team. He's investigating evidence, asking questions, and making deductions. I really don't think friendship comes into the equation," said Cherry. "They could think that I'm a very polished criminal who does these dastardly deeds under the radar and then continues acting like a common, everyday Graceland docent."

Lulu got the impression that Cherry was possibly enjoying being a suspect. That had to mean that she really didn't think the police were seriously considering her as the murderer.

They heard male voices approaching the porch from the street and Lulu glanced at her watch. "That should be Derrick and Finn. Morty hasn't gotten here yet. Hmm."

"Hopefully he's not dead," intoned Cherry mischievously.

Lulu frowned at her. "Certainly not. Morty isn't even on the periphery of this case."

"I'm just saying—things are heating up. We never know who's going to be the next victim," said Cherry.

Lulu didn't have time to respond to that because it was Finn and Derrick and they were up on the porch and standing next to them in a couple of long strides. Cherry did a quick hi-and-bye because it was time for her to go run errands and do yard work. After she left, Derrick said, "Granny Lulu, is it all right if we put together some snacks in the kitchen?"

"That's fine with me as long as you stay out of Ben's way . . . he'll be trying to clean up from lunch and get things ready for supper. There should be lots of snack possibilities in there," said Lulu, trying to recollect the contents for the family fridge—separate from the industrial-size fridge they used for the restaurant.

"Is there maybe any pink lemonade pie in there?" asked Derrick, trying to act innocent.

Lulu laughed. "Was it you, then, that got into my pie? I noticed when I came in that it wasn't in the same condition I'd left it in yesterday."

"What condition had you left it in yesterday?" asked Finn.

"Uneaten," said Lulu, smiling.

"I might have had one slice of pie, just to see if I liked it," said Derrick, a smile playing around his lips. "So Ben's trying to work in there right now? How about I grab the pie and plates and forks and Finn and I knock it out first. Do you mind?"

"I don't. As a matter of fact, I did remember that I had a hungry teenager on the premises here on school days and I took the precaution of making a whole other pie for the twins when they come in. I hid it under a couple of bags of lettuce," said Lulu smugly.

"Has it come to that?" asked Derrick, laughing. "To the point where you have to hide food?"

"Oh, I think so," said Lulu. "The rest of us need to be able to eat, too!"

As Derrick laughed and walked off to the kitchen for the lemonade pie, Lulu smiled after him. It wasn't all that long ago when Derrick wasn't comfortable enough to joke around with everyone. He'd come to them insecure, defensive, and nearly silent. She was so happy to see that the warm, loving, and accepting atmosphere of the restaurant had worked its magic on Derrick. He still had plenty of insecurity, but it seemed like he was getting more confident every day.

Now she turned to Finn to ask him about his day when she caught him with a wistful expression on his face. "Everything okay, Finn? Why don't you have a seat next to me while we wait on the food?"

"It's just—well, it's nice to see everybody acting so normal," said Finn. "At home we're never that relaxed. I'm uptight, Mom's uptight. It's not a fun place like this is."

Lulu said, "Sweetie, I'm sorry things have been so rough for you. And you know you're welcome to hang out here with us as much as you'd like, as long as it's okay with your mom. You know your mother has been under a lot of stress lately and that's got a lot to do with it."

Finn gave a laugh that was more like a groan. "Believe me, I know all about her stress over money. That's all Mom talks about!"

Lulu nodded quietly, figuring that Finn needed somebody to just listen to him.

"I've tried to be good on my end, but it's tough. I try to help out around the house or do the things that Mom wants me to do that Dad would have done when they were together—stuff like clearing out a clogged pipe or mowing the grass, or stuff like that," said Finn.

"Y'all own a house?" asked Lulu.

"No, we're renting one. A duplex, I guess it is. It's pretty small, but a decent size for us. But it's nice to get away from there and come here to hang out some," said Finn.

Lulu asked delicately, "And y'all have been getting along with each other okay?"

Finn shrugged. "It's been okay. Sometimes we fight with each other, but it's not a lot. The last time was a big argument we had a couple of weeks ago. For the first time, when I came home, there was a guy in the driveway. She even introduced him to me—a guy named John. I figured it was somebody she was trying to date . . . and I guess I wasn't ready. As soon as he drove off, she and I really had it out."

Lulu was very still. There were a lot of Johns in the world. But in this case, everybody seemed like they were connected. She said, "That's only natural, Finn. That's a huge adjustment for you. Besides, you were probably trying to take care of your mama and protect her. I was wondering if John was someone that I knew—what did he look like, if you can remember?"

And Finn described the same John. Right down to the stripe of white hair on his head. The same John that Dawn had just finished telling her that she didn't know.

"You didn't see him again after that, though?" asked Lulu.

Finn's shoulders relaxed. "No, I sure didn't. Mom probably had second thoughts or something, after we had that argument. I'm really not trying to control her life or anything—I was taken by surprise by the whole thing, I guess. I sort of feel guilty about it now."

Lulu reached over to hug the boy. "Honey, you shouldn't worry about it. Your mama loves and cares about you. Did you know that she was here a little while ago? She wanted to check and see that your trumpet lessons were safe. She sure does care a lot about you."

She had the satisfaction of seeing Finn's face brighten. Then Derrick arrived on the porch with the pie and Morty arrived with his trumpet and Lulu retreated to the office to get some work done.

Lulu ended up visiting with regulars in the dining room, even helping to wait on tables when they got busy over supper. Then she helped sweep up when it was time to clean. They'd put the closed sign outside when Pink showed up.

The policeman said, "Lulu, is it okay if we talk now? I know you've got to be tired out from working all day."

Ben and Sara were on their way to leave when they hesitated. "Do you need us to stay, Lulu?" asked Sara.

"Heavens, no!" said Lulu. "Pink and I are going to catch up a little bit about these murders. Y'all go on home—you've got to be tired. And I know the twins and Derrick are long asleep."

"Okay," said Ben. "Tim is here still, by the way. You know he came back to the restaurant to help clean up? Although he worked a full shift today."

"He didn't finish his shift yesterday, so he wanted to put in some extra time tonight, that's all," said Lulu.

Ben and Sara left, locking the door behind them, and Pink and Lulu settled across from each other in a booth. "I guess we both have the kind of jobs where we're on our feet all day," said Pink ruefully. "I never turn down the opportunity to sit for a spell."

Lulu made her usual offers of food and drinks and Pink turned her down this time. "I appreciate it, Lulu, but I'm good. I'm here to check in with you on what you've found out with these murders I'm investigating."

Lulu smiled at him. "So you're not here to tell me that you've arrested Cherry, then. She seemed happily convinced that everyone thought she might be a villain."

"I don't think the focus of our investigation is Cherry. We'd all be completely shocked if she was behind these murders," said Pink.

"She'll be crushed to hear that," said Lulu with a chuckle. "So you're checking in to see what she and I have found out?"

"That's right. Not that I approve of y'all getting involved in this in any way—let me go on the record saying that. It's far too dangerous. As long as y'all are getting information in a natural way—through normal interactions with people you're associated with—then I don't mind finding out what I can from you," said Pink.

Lulu nodded. "Honestly, Pink, I don't know what information I have to give you. It all seems like a mess.

Besides, you probably know all the information that I've got."

"Well, tell me what you've learned, and if it duplicates what we know, then that's okay. I'd rather hear it all anyway," said Pink. "By the way, it seems like you've been spending a lot of time lately with two of my suspects—Brody and Sharon."

"Sharon has gotten to be friendly with Cherry and me, and Brody has, too. Why? Is there something we should know?" asked Lulu, frowning. "Sharon is an emotional wreck most of the time and seems completely stressed out. Brody is pretty easy-going and seems to balance Sharon out. They both seem nice."

"Possibly they are. Very possibly. But then, there's always the possibility that they're homicidal maniacs, too. I will tell you one thing, Lulu—those two are in a financial mess. They've lived beyond their means for way too long. I'm not even sure how they duped a bank into giving them a mortgage. They've got debt up to their eyeballs. That money they got from Reuben's will is a real godsend for them," said Pink pointedly.

"I'll be sure to keep an eye on my pocketbook when I'm around them," said Lulu with a sassy wink. She didn't mention that she wasn't at all surprised to hear that Sharon and Brody were having financial trouble. Sharon's older designer clothes and purse, and the unfinished appearance of the house, definitely indicated they were trying not to spend a lot of money.

Pink sighed. "All right. But don't say I didn't warn you. Now that I've shared some information, can you return the favor?"

"I really do think you already heard it all, Pink. Like the fact that Reuben Shaw's ex-wife has financial problems and health issues and was mad at Reuben because he didn't help out. And the fact that Reuben died a rich man, because his uncle died not long before Reuben was murdered. And . . ." She hesitated. Because Pink probably didn't know about Tim. And Lulu wasn't sure she was the one who should be telling that story.

Someone cleared his throat behind them. They turned around to see Tim. Pink frowned at the waiter in confusion, which didn't make Tim any more relaxed.

"Pink, you know Tim, don't you?" asked Lulu.

Pink's eyebrows were drawn together still. "Well, sure. Tim brings me barbeque plates almost every day."

Tim's hands shook. "I'm here because I want to make a confession."

Now Lulu was staring at Tim, too. Was he going to own up to his connection with Reuben and the hit-and-run involvement from his past? Or was he going to confess to two murders?

Chapter
14

Tim cleared his throat. "You don't know this, Pink, but I'm connected to Reuben Shaw. He and I used to be friends a couple of years back. But then he got to drinking and we were out one night two years ago. He was driving a car that was involved in a fatal hit-and-run. I was the passenger who didn't make him stop."

Tim looked like he might fall over, so Lulu motioned him to sit beside her at the booth. He quickly did.

Pink was thinking back. "I believe I do recollect an unresolved hit-and-run from a few years ago. Family man, wasn't it?"

Tim turned green. The subject was still very raw for him.

"But you weren't driving, you say? And the person

who *was* driving is dead. And we don't even know where the car is that he was driving?" asked Pink.

Tim said, "He might still have it in his garage or something. I know I never saw him drive it after that, but he and I stopped talking after that night."

Pink was still mulling this all over. "You didn't report an accident."

"In fact, I encouraged the driver to leave the scene," said Tim in as brave a tone as he could muster.

"Right." Pink sighed. "I'm going to need to report this and probably have the officers who were assigned to that case come talk with you, if they're still on the force. But honestly? I don't think you're going to be held accountable for this. You weren't driving the car. We don't have any evidence that you're lying about that. So ultimately, the choice to stop was taken out of your hands."

"I'll tell the police everything I remember about that night," said Tim. "And it's still pretty clear in my head."

"I know you said that you and Reuben weren't speaking to each other," said Pink. "But had you been in touch with him recently? And did you have anything to do with his death?"

Tim stared down at the table. "I did get back in touch with him. I told him that I'd hit rock bottom and wanted to confess to my part in that accident. Reuben didn't want anything to do with a confession. Once he realized that I was going to the police even if he didn't turn himself in, he kept trying to contact me. He even found out I was working here and called for me at work. We ran into each other at the festival and he started yelling at me, trying to convince me to keep my mouth shut."

Pink raised his eyebrows. "So you saw Reuben at the festival? When was it that you saw him?"

Tim sighed, studying the table's wood surface as if it were the most interesting thing in the world. "From what I understand, I saw him not long before he was murdered." Now he stared Pink in the eye. "But I didn't have anything to do with his death. All I wanted to do was to come clean. The last thing I wanted was another death on my hands."

Pink nodded, like he was satisfied. "Okay. I'll pull up the hit-and-run incident when I get back to the station. I'm sure some guys from the department will be getting in touch with you." He wearily rubbed his eyes. "I'm done for the day," he said, standing up to take his leave.

Tim's face was relieved. "I'd better go, too. You coming, Mrs. Taylor?"

"I've got to finish up in the office and lock up. Y'all go ahead. I'll be a few minutes behind you," said Lulu.

Lulu walked toward the parking deck where she'd left her car. This was Beale Street, and even though it was late, the nightlife was only starting up. Music spilled out from the restaurants and bars and people were walking up the street holding drinks and laughing with each other. Like the Rock and Ribs festival, Beale Street gave off a real party atmosphere.

There were gobs of people outside. As usual, Lulu felt

perfectly safe—or as safe as it was possible to feel. Was there ever a time in modern life when you were walking by yourself that you didn't think about your personal safety just a smidge?

Lulu paid attention to her surroundings, she later remembered, as she walked, although she was thinking about the murders. She'd turned off the street and had barely set foot in the parking deck when she felt something smashing into the back of her head. And aside from that, a strange musical sound that accompanied the strike.

The next thing she saw, and she was thankful to be alive to see it, was Tim's face, peering at her with great concern.

"Mrs. Taylor! Are you okay?" His anxious face swam woozily before her and she tried to focus on one of the Tims she saw.

She didn't like anybody to worry about her and she tried reassuring him, but all that came out was a grunt.

Tim swung around to peer behind him and Lulu heard the sound of a car. "Hold on. I think that's Pink leaving." He left her side.

This time it was Pink's face she saw, and it was grim. "Lulu, I'm going to call you an ambulance."

Now this was something she tried harder to react to. "No," she managed to groan. "No hospital."

Tim and Pink exchanged glances. Pink said, "Lulu, you had a pretty big smack to the back of your head. You might even have a concussion."

Lulu quickly gave them the current year and current president.

Tim gave a relieved laugh and Pink said, "All right, well, I guess you passed that test. Maybe you don't have a concussion."

Lulu was starting to feel less dizzy, which meant that her head was starting to hurt. "I just want to go home. Can y'all help get me home?"

Tim said to Pink, "I could drive Mrs. Taylor's car if you drive me back here to get mine afterwards."

Lulu said, "That's too much trouble, y'all. Tim, you've had a long day on your feet at the restaurant. If Pink will drop me off at the house, then I can get a ride to Aunt Pat's tomorrow morning from Cherry or somebody. No worries."

So that's what they did. Once she stood up, she was a lot more unsteady than she thought. Good thing she wasn't driving. Pink offered his arm to her and guided her to the police car.

As they were driving to Lulu's house, Pink said, "I guess you didn't see or hear anything that would give us any clues?"

Lulu tried to remember. Now she really couldn't recollect anything in those few minutes even before she was hit in the head. Not that she was going to share that with Pink or else she might end up spending the night at the hospital, which was not what she wanted. "No, I don't think I did," she said ruefully. "I was being careful, though—I'm always careful when I leave the restaurant at night. But I've been making that trek for many years now and never had a problem."

"They didn't take your purse," Pink pointed out. "And you don't have any contents of your purse missing, do you?"

He turned on the car's interior lights for her and Lulu made a perfunctory search of her pocketbook. She knew that she hadn't been mugged, though. She had the strong feeling that she'd been warned. Still, she rummaged through her bag. She had the cheerful makeup bag with the powder and the pink lipstick. She had her fat wallet that was fair to bursting with quarters. She had her cell phone. A baggie of dog treats for the restaurant's Labs. A pack of tissues, a pair of plastic sunglasses, her keys. "Everything is here," she reported.

It felt like there was an important detail that she was missing. But she couldn't remember what it was.

Lulu said, "I'm so lucky that y'all were still hanging around. Did Tim say if he got a glimpse of the person who attacked me?"

Pink shook his head as he drove her through the dark streets. "He didn't. He was driving out of the parking deck when he saw you lying on the ground."

"So it wasn't like the attack was interrupted then," said Lulu. Somebody must be trying to scare her. But why? Did someone think she was getting too close to the truth? It sure didn't feel that way.

Pink said, echoing her thoughts, "Now I know you told me tonight that you didn't know anything. I need you to try and think back . . . are you *certain* you don't? Because it looks like somebody thinks you do."

"No, now that you know about Tim, you know everything that I do," said Lulu. "And I don't think somebody was trying to knock me off tonight. I guess this takes Tim off the list of suspects, too."

"No, if somebody wanted to kill you tonight, you'd be dead. Because whoever this killer is, they're good. I know you're used to walking back to your car by yourself, but you need to take extra precautions until this case is wrapped up."

Lulu frowned. "Like what? You're not wanting me to pack heat or anything."

Pink snorted. "Like you would, even if I asked you to. No, but think ahead. Try not to walk alone, be alert to your surroundings, draw attention to an attack, react quickly, and fight back hard. You know."

Lulu did. But she didn't usually think that way, she had to admit.

"I'm guessing this person wants you to back off. And I think that might be a good plan, Lulu. You're my friend and I don't want to lose you."

Lulu misted up just a little.

"Besides," Pink drawled, "how would I get my daily fix of ribs?" He turned to give Lulu a wink and she laughed.

"And Lulu," said Pink, getting serious again. "You crossed Tim off your list of suspects, but he could have been the one to whack you over the head before he conveniently discovered you. Don't feel too safe around *any*body."

The next morning, Lulu felt every single one of her sixty-odd years. You'd think it would only be her head that hurt, but instead it seemed like she hurt all over. Falling down must have caused more bruising than she thought.

She felt better after soaking in the tub and taking a couple of ibuprofen. The headache she'd woken up with, though, didn't want to go away.

Around lunch, she decided she might forget her aches and pains more if she drove over to Aunt Pat's. At least there would be distractions there, and if she didn't feel like waiting on tables or talking to customers in the dining room, she could sit on the porch and greet folks as they came in.

She smiled when she walked onto the front porch at Aunt Pat's and saw Morty, Buddy, and Big Ben there. "Exactly who I was hoping to see!" said Lulu, giving them hugs.

Buddy peered at her. "Say, you're looking peaked, Lulu. Are those bruises I'm seeing?"

Lulu's son, naturally, came out on the porch right about that time. "Mother?" asked Ben. "What happened to you?"

Lulu sighed. On the one hand, it felt really good to

have people who cared so much about her. On the other, it was tough when they hovered. And there was definitely hovering going on now.

"I'm fine, y'all," she said in what she hoped was a convincing voice. "I had a little incident last night, that's all. A few bruises and a headache, but other than that, I'm fit as a fiddle."

Ben came closer, studying her carefully. "You're all bruised up! What on earth happened, Mother? And— last night? You were fine when I left you at the restaurant last night. You even had a policeman with you! How could anything have happened to you last night?"

Lulu told Ben and her friends what happened in as matter-of-fact a way as possible. If she was going to get to the bottom of this mess, it sure was going to be hard to do if Ben had her on lockdown for her own safety. "We don't know what exactly the motivation was," she said with what she hoped was a careless shrug. "It could have been a random act of violence. Or someone watching for an opportunity to steal something."

"Was anything stolen?" Ben demanded, arms crossed.

"Well . . . no. But Tim was on the scene so quickly that maybe my attacker got spooked and wanted to get out of there before he was caught," said Lulu.

Ben, Morty, Buddy, and Big Ben looked at one another.

Morty said slowly, "Doesn't it seem coincidental that you'd get attacked while you're trying to check out what's going on with these murders?"

"Awfully coincidental, I'd think," said Buddy, nodding.

"It might seem that way, but think about it," said Lulu. "If this murderer wanted to get rid of me, don't you think he would have? Like Pink said, this guy is good at what he does—there's already two bodies he's responsible for. Why wouldn't he finish off the job?"

"Maybe he wanted to scare you off," said Ben. "I know he's scaring me off. You need to stop nosing around on this case. Pink is a great cop. He's going to figure out what's going on and send him off to jail. I hate to think what might have happened last night. What if Tim hadn't been there to find you?" asked Ben. "What would have happened then?"

"Well, I don't really know. I guess Pink might have spotted me," said Lulu.

"Not likely. Sounds like he was on the other side of the parking deck and only came over because Tim flagged him down," said Ben.

"You and Sara would have seen me," said Lulu, frowning.

"No, remember, we'd already left for the night before you came out," said Ben.

Lulu kept frowning. "Well, then, I guess I'd have woken up on my own and gradually gotten in the car and driven myself home."

"With a really bad headache," said Ben with a sigh. "Do you see where I'm going with this?"

"Not really," admitted Lulu.

"Did you even have your cell phone with you?" asked Ben.

"I surely did!" said Lulu quickly.

"Do you have it on you now?" asked Ben.

Lulu reached into her oversized pocketbook and pulled out the offending item. She had an active dislike for cell phones. It distressed her to see folks at Aunt Pat's talking on their phones instead of visiting with the friends who were at the table with them. She'd never taken to the things, and barely tolerated having one in her purse.

Ben took it and pushed the power button. It made no signs of coming to life.

He solemnly stared at Lulu. "Mother, it appears that the battery needs to be charged."

"Why would it need to be charged if I don't turn it on?"

"Well, after a while, the battery still needs charging. And you need to keep the phone on anyway—remember that I told you that emergencies go both ways?" asked Ben.

Lulu sighed. "I know. I meant to have it on. I guess I'm just not in the habit. And I'm not real fond of talking on the phone anyway. When I call people, I always feel like I'm interrupting them in the middle of something important."

"We've all got text plans," said Ben. "Maybe Derrick can show you how to text. That way you're not even talking on the phone, you're typing on it. It doesn't interrupt people like a phone call does. I know how you feel about interruptions."

"Derrick seems so busy lately," said Lulu, feeling doubtful. "I know he's around some, but I still don't see him nearly as much as I used to."

Ben said, "Does it seem to y'all like he's got some sort of secret? A couple of times he's left the restaurant in a rush and wasn't real clear where he was going or who he was hanging out with."

Lulu's heart sank. "I've thought the same thing, but I didn't want to say anything."

Morty said drily, "Know what? His secret is probably that he's a teenager and doesn't want adults messing about in his business. Don't worry about it—Derrick is a great kid with a good head on his shoulders. Teenagers always are cagey when you try to nail down where they're heading. And if he doesn't have a chance to show you how to text on your phone, then I can show you, Lulu. I told you that I'm hip to that kind of stuff."

Buddy said, "Going back to what we were talking about, the whole reason you were asking questions and nosing around was that you were trying to make sure that Cherry wasn't a suspect, isn't that right? You wanted to clear her name, wasn't that what Morty was telling me?" He finished off his barbeque plate.

"That's right," said Lulu. "Plus the fact that I did discover the body."

Ben said, "I can't imagine that anybody would take Cherry seriously as a suspect. She's too flaky."

"Hey!" said a belligerent voice and Cherry opened

the porch door. "Y'all are talking about me behind my back. I would too make a good murder suspect!"

"Not really," said Morty. "Maybe you might murder *one* person. I sure can't picture you murdering two."

Buddy said, "She acts like she wants to murder her Johnny sometimes." He laughed.

"Besides, Cherry would definitely not be responsible for attacking you last night," said Ben. "I mean—really. Do you really believe Pink will think that Cherry would lie in wait to kill you?"

"What?" asked Cherry, wide-eyed with alarm.

Of course they'd had to fill Cherry in. This time, at least, it was Ben telling the story with Lulu adding bits here and there. Lulu had the feeling this was a story she was going to quickly tire of telling.

Ben wrapped up the tale. "So that's why I was saying that I couldn't imagine Pink would consider you a suspect, Cherry. And why Mother should stop snooping where someone obviously doesn't like it."

Cherry said, "It's going to be hard for Lulu to stop. But I can make sure I'm with her. I'm supposed to be her sidekick," she said pointedly. "Although sometimes your mama wants to do things all by herself."

"It just turns out that way," protested Lulu. "Sometimes I stumble into things when I'm alone—I don't plan for it to happen. I sure didn't plan on being hit over the head last night. I was minding my own business last night anyway."

"I think having you as a sidekick is a good plan," said Morty. He said to Ben in a reasonable voice, "You don't think a murderer could take on both of them, do you? This isn't the Mafia we're talking about. It's somebody who got annoyed with Reuben and then needed to cover his tracks by killing someone who knew too much."

"I guess so," said Ben. He still didn't seem too tickled about it.

A change of subject was in order. "Ben, how are things going in the kitchen? I haven't seen you at all lately," said Lulu.

Ben shook his head. "It's been completely nuts. I really need someone else to help me out. I've got one other cook, as you know, but splitting the work between the two of us is still making for too much work. I could use another part-time hand or even more than part-time."

"That's a sign that business is doing good," drawled Buddy. "I can think of worse problems to have."

Tim joined Ben on the porch. "Mrs. Taylor? I was checking in and wanted to see how you were doing." He was carrying a grocery bag.

"Mrs. Taylor?" Morty glanced around him in mock confusion. "I don't see any Mrs. Taylor out here, do y'all?"

Lulu laughed. "He's right, Tim. Just call me Lulu, like I asked you before. Everybody else does. And I'm fine, thanks for asking. A lot more fine than I would have been if I'd woken up by myself in that parking deck."

Ben held out his hand and said, "Tim, I want to thank

you for seeing to my mother last night. I understand that you're the one who found her and flagged down Pink. I really appreciate it."

Tim colored faintly. "I'm glad that I noticed her lying there when I was leaving. I really didn't do anything. Except—I did want to tell you, or I guess Pink, about something that I remembered after I got home last night. When I was on my way out to my car, I did notice Brody's truck."

Lulu's breath caught. "You did? I didn't know you'd recognize Brody's truck."

"Of course, I didn't actually know Brody from when Reuben and I were hanging out, but I recognized him from all the pictures with them together—hunting and fishing trips and all. And I did see Brody getting into his truck a few times at the festival when he was setting up the booth," said Tim.

Morty frowned. "Wouldn't there be tons of trucks that look the same, though? How'd you know it was his?"

"His really stands out—it's a mustard yellow color. If it wasn't his truck, it sure resembled it," said Tim.

Could Brody have been behind her attack? Making sure she backed off with her investigating? She hated to think so. But somebody sure wanted to scare her and it had to be one of the folks who were suspects. "Thanks for letting me know, Tim. I'll pass that info along to Pink, too, the very next time I see him."

Tim flushed. "Oh, speaking of Pink—he called me

early today to say there was no problem with the other thing. You know. From a couple of years ago. So now I'm just going to plan on contacting the family directly and see how I can help apologize to them." He gave a shy smile as Lulu reached over to hug him.

"Here you are being all cryptic again, Lulu," said Buddy with a sigh. "Sometimes I think I never know what's going on."

"Join the club," bellowed Big Ben.

Tim cleared his throat. "Mrs.—Lulu—I'm glad you're feeling better." He reached into the grocery bag and pulled out a plate wrapped with aluminum foil. "I wasn't sure if you'd be in today or not, but I figured something sweet might help."

He pulled off the foil to reveal mini cheesecakes. Lulu clapped her hands.

"Oh, you've done it now!" said Ben, laughing. "Mother will have to adopt you and make you an honorary son. She might even disown me in favor of you. Cheesecake is one of her favorite desserts."

"I think it might be my most favorite," said Lulu. "The only problem is that usually I have to cut myself a slice off the pie, and I can't stop myself from cutting off a huge piece. With these little mini cheesecakes, I can have a taste and then be good and put the plate back in the fridge. Like this."

Lulu reached out to demonstrate eating only one. The cheesecake was absolutely amazing and melted in her mouth. "Mmm," she said. "Heavenly. Chocolate chip cheesecake!"

Ben said, "Hey, do you mind if I have a small bite, Tim? Only a nibble, because if everybody has a bite, then there won't be any left for Mother." He took an experimental bite, chewing thoughtfully. "So Tim," he said, "you mentioned that you liked baking. Do you do a lot of cooking?"

Tim nodded, looking at Ben quizzically. "I used to. When I had more time and . . . well, more money, I guess."

"I know you've done a great job helping us wait on tables while you've been here," said Ben. "But now I'm thinking your talents might be wasted on serving food. Want to try spending time in the kitchen with me? If it works out for both of us, maybe we can work out a cooking shift for you. For more pay, of course."

Tim's face lit up. "That would be great, Mr. Taylor."

"There he goes again," said Morty in a dry voice.

"Just Ben is fine, Tim," said Ben. He glanced at his watch. "I've got to run. Time to start cooking. Mother, do we have enough waiters to help out today? Can I steal Tim for a while?"

Tim's face was a bit panicked at his sudden drafting. Ben quickly added, "Just to do some chopping for me— stuff like that."

"We're probably covered, Ben," said Lulu.

They disappeared into the dining room and Lulu smiled. "Well, I hope that turns out okay. Tim could sure use a break. He's had a real rough time." She glanced across the porch and frowned. "That's not one of y'all's jackets, is it?" she asked Morty, Buddy, and Big Ben.

They shook their heads and Morty said, "You know, I think that belongs to my friend, Finn."

"Are y'all meeting today after school?" asked Lulu.

Morty said, "Not today. Finn has some kind of big project or essay or something due. In fact, I don't think we're meeting again until next week."

"Maybe I should run it out to their house, then," said Lulu. "In case it's something he likes to wear at school."

"Or so he doesn't get in trouble with his mama for losing it," said Morty, rolling his eyes. "She's pretty rough to live with, according to Finn."

"And she's a possible murderer, to boot," said Big Ben in his booming voice.

"I hope she's not," said Morty. "She's all he's got, flawed or not."

Lulu found that they did need an extra server for supper. She stayed to wait on the tables and sit down and chat with her diners for a spell. When she had a chance to breathe and glance at her watch, she was surprised to see that it was already eight thirty. She didn't want to startle Dawn by ringing her doorbell too late, so she quickly grabbed her pocketbook and told Ben and Sara that she was heading out.

"Be careful, Mother!" Ben shouted out behind her as she let the kitchen door swing shut behind her.

Chapter 15

Lulu did pay particular attention on her way to her car. She wasn't going to give anybody the pleasure of making her feel scared, though. She wasn't scared—but she was definitely on high alert. There seemed to be more shadows and hiding places on her familiar route to the parking deck than there usually were. When she made it to her car, she locked the doors quickly after she'd gotten inside.

The drive to Dawn's house didn't take long. She and Finn were renting a duplex-style house that was clearly an older home, but appeared carefully kept up. The light was fading fast when Lulu parked in their driveway so she grabbed the jacket and hurried to the front door.

The curtain at the window beside the door fluttered

after Lulu rang the bell, then Dawn opened the door. "I'm running by Finn's jacket. He accidentally left it at Aunt Pat's and I wanted to make sure he got it back in case he needed it for school."

Dawn reached out for the jacket. Her gaze registered Lulu's injuries, but she didn't say anything about them. "Thanks," she said. "I know it seems really hot to have a jacket, but the school is real cold, he says—the air conditioner is blasting all the time. He likes to wear it during the day. Thanks for bringing it over for him."

There was a short, musical burst that made Lulu's blood run cold. "What's that?" she gasped, not knowing why it made her feel so scared.

Dawn stared curiously at her. "Just my cell phone. That's the sound it makes when I get a text message." She pulled the phone out of her pocket and glanced at it.

That sound that her cell phone made was the sound Lulu had heard when she'd been attacked in the parking deck.

"Can I ask you something?" said Lulu, swallowing down her fear. "What were you doing last night?"

"Last night?" asked Dawn, raising her eyebrows in surprise. "I was here at home. Had a headache last night, so I went to bed early."

"Finn was here, too?" asked Lulu.

"No, actually, he wasn't. He and another kid from school are working on a group project for their history class. That's where he is now and where he was last night. He let himself in with a key, since I was sound asleep whenever it was when he got home. Why do you ask?" said Dawn, frowning now.

Lulu told the story about her attack last night again and Dawn's eyes widened and her gaze fell back on Lulu's bruises, which were now turning the color of autumn leaves. "No," said Dawn, "I didn't know anything about that. I guess we should all be watching our step now. Do you want to come inside for a few minutes?"

No, she really didn't. Especially since she'd recognized the sound of Dawn's phone. The doorstep was good enough.

"No, I'm good. I should be heading back home to go to bed early. One more question for you, if you don't mind," said Lulu.

Dawn shrugged but looked behind her impatiently as if she wanted to go back to her TV show or whatever she'd been doing before Lulu showed up.

"Finn mentioned that you knew John—the man who was one of Reuben's customers and wasn't pleased with the job Reuben was doing. The one I told you had been murdered," said Lulu. "But you said you didn't know him. Finn said John was in your driveway one day when he came home."

Dawn said, "No, I *didn't* know him at all. And I didn't realize that's who you were talking about. John is a very common name, you know. Finn misread the situation. Yes, that John did come by here. He'd been spending a lot of time trying to figure out how to force Reuben to finish the work on his house—work that he said he'd already paid for. He found out about the divorce and heard that I wasn't happy with Reuben, either. He came to the house to see if he and I could somehow join forces and put pressure on Reuben."

"What kind of pressure?" asked Lulu.

"I have no idea. I didn't want anything to do with it. I was going to keep laying guilt trips on Reuben and see if I could get somewhere by doing that. I wasn't sure what this John was up to, but I thought he might want to do something shady somehow. Like blackmail or something. I've got Finn depending on me for everything and I didn't want to do something stupid that might put me in jail," said Dawn.

Lulu hesitated, then said, "Someone mentioned seeing you near Reuben's booth the night he was killed. I guess the police have probably asked you about that, too. But you weren't trying to snoop around and find dirt on Reuben?"

Dawn rolled her eyes. "What *haven't* they asked me about? Yes, I stupidly went over there when I finally realized he was at the festival. Somebody I know spotted him there. Believe me, I regret being anywhere in the vicinity because it's caused nothing but trouble for me. I wanted to see if I could drag Reuben away for a minute or two and give him a piece of my mind. Unfortunately, he wasn't around. I guess he was off getting murdered.

No, I wasn't following John's directions and trying to get dirt on Reuben, I was only trying to find him to yell at him."

She still spoke of her ex-husband's death with real ice in her voice. Lulu cleared her throat. "So you thought that's what John was wanting you to do? Dig up dirt on Reuben or something?" asked Lulu.

"He thought there was something in Reuben's past that might be good to pressure him with. If there was, I don't know about it," said Dawn. "All I know is that he changed. Some people change over the years and some people change overnight. Reuben's change was the overnight variety."

"Have you heard anything about the will being settled? Are things going to get better for you and Finn? It'd be nice if something good could come out of all this," said Lulu.

Dawn shrugged. "I hear things. It sounds like maybe Finn's future is looking up. It had to—anything was better than being broke. Maybe Finn can go to a decent college or something. He won't be in the same mess that I'm in anyway. But yeah, Reuben's old uncle finally passed. He was always talking about the old boy, bragging about him. Whenever we visited him, I wasn't all that impressed with the uncle, let me tell you. He wore these tatty old clothes and always seemed like he needed a shave. He didn't sound like he'd had much school, either. So I thought Reuben was full of a lot of hot air."

"But he wasn't?" asked Lulu.

"Apparently not. So now Finn has money to go to school or to get started in the world. Of course, I'm out of luck because Reuben and I were already divorced." She had a considering sort of expression on her face that made Lulu wonder if maybe she was going to wrangle that money away from Finn.

The moment passed, though. Dawn slowly said, "You know, I'm just glad that Finn is going to be okay. I worried about that kid all the time. My health issues and bills . . . yeah, they're a pain. But Finn was the one that kept me up at night and kept me pounding on Reuben's door, asking him for money all the time. I'm glad things will work out for him. It takes a lot of pressure off me, let me tell you."

"Was Finn the only beneficiary for Reuben's will?" Lulu hoped she sounded like she didn't already know the answer to that question.

Dawn's face was set once again into angry lines. "No," she said in a clipped voice. "He sure wasn't. Should've been. But wasn't. Look, I got to go. That headache of mine is coming back."

Lulu's nerves were still jangling after hearing the sound that Dawn's phone had made. She recognized it as the sound she'd heard during her attack. Could Dawn have been behind the attack? Or was it someone else who had the same texting ringtone?

Going home didn't seem all that appealing. The way

her mind was spinning, she needed someone to help re-center her so that she could wind down and maybe get some sleep. Cherry. Maybe Cherry's brand of straight talk could help ground her again.

Lulu glanced at her watch. It was pretty late now, though—after nine thirty. She better call her first.

"What? Well, sure, hon, come on over. I've got a glass of wine with your name on it. Don't let me scare you when I open the door," said Cherry. "You'll see what I mean."

Lulu did. Cherry had on a green oatmeal mask and wore a scarlet shower cap, probably to keep the oatmeal out of her hair. She gave Lulu a hug and transferred some of the green glop with it. She'd seen Cherry in her beauty treatments before, but the effect was still quite startling. "You look stressed, sweetie. Come on in and we'll have a cool beverage."

"Is Johnny around?" asked Lulu. She saw neither hide nor hair of him but was sure he'd have his usual grim air of resignation whenever he was around Cherry. He was diametrically opposite from her in every way and spent most of his time giving her baleful or confused stares as if wondering how he'd ended up with such a spitfire.

"No, he's in Mississippi, visiting his people." Cherry seemed relieved that she wasn't with him. Apparently, Johnny's Mississippi kin weren't all that fascinating to be around. "What's going on?" she demanded, pouring

Lulu a healthy glass of wine that ensured a fairly long visit for Lulu for the alcohol to wear off.

Just being in Cherry's house helped Lulu relax. It was as colorful as she was. Cherry had hung posters of Elvis everywhere—all from his black-and-white heyday—and she had several pictures of motorcycles on the walls, too. Lulu sat down on a bright red sofa with black pillows that made the couch resemble a ladybug.

Lulu filled her in on her visit to Dawn.

"You weren't supposed to be doing anything risky!" said Cherry, eyebrows knitting on her green face.

"I was only returning a jacket, Cherry!" protested Lulu. "I didn't think I was doing anything besides being thoughtful, I promise."

"You're edging me out of this case," said Cherry, hands on her hips and green face stern.

"Not one bit. I always want to hear your opinions on things. That's why I'm here right now. Besides, you're the whole reason I'm even involved in all this mess. You were the one who invited me over to the Graces' tent. You were with me when we found the body. And you were one of the original suspects," said Lulu.

"I guess you're right," said Cherry, mollified. "I'm too important to try to work around. So . . . what are you thinking? Was it Dawn's cell phone that you heard before you were attacked?"

"I don't know," said Lulu, wishing she could be sure.

"It was the same ringtone, but I guess a lot of people could use the same one."

"What about Finn?" suggested Cherry. "Do you think his mom might have been texting him when he was fixing to strike at you?"

Lulu took a big sip of her wine. Then she said, "Cherry, I simply can't imagine why Finn would do something like that. What makes you think it could have been him?"

"Well, teenagers text like crazy, you know," said Cherry. "I keep hearing on the news how they have all these texting-related injuries."

"That's what I hear, too. But why do you think Finn would kill his dad, and somebody he didn't even know, and attack me?" asked Lulu.

"In my way of thinking," said Cherry, gesturing with her wineglass until it sloshed over into her lap, "Finn knew that he was going to come into some money. It's not easy being poor. I've been poor before and there was nothing genteel about it, let me tell you. Maybe he's also got hurt feelings because his dad deserted him and his mom. You hear about these kinds of stories on the news, too."

"But Finn probably thought his dad didn't even have any money," said Lulu. "After all, he wasn't working. Dawn said Reuben was hanging out all day in a bathrobe."

"Maybe during one of those super-rare parental

visits, Reuben bragged to Finn that his uncle had died and that he was getting a bunch of money," said Cherry. "Reuben would have to know that Finn would go right to Dawn with that information. It would have been a great way to get back at Dawn—if Reuben were rich, that would have made her furious."

"But Dawn said that Reuben never really saw Finn and wasn't doing the visits he was supposed to," said Lulu.

"Maybe she's trying to cover up for Finn," said Cherry with a shrug. "Or maybe she's covering up for herself."

"What about John?" asked Lulu. "You think Finn killed him because he knew too much? Maybe when John was sneaking around trying to dig up dirt on Reuben, he saw Finn attacking his dad?"

Cherry said, "Or Dawn was right and Finn totally misread the whole situation when he drove up that day and saw John and his mom together. Maybe Finn was trying to protect his mother. Maybe John saw *Dawn* killing Reuben and was blackmailing her."

"What if Finn wasn't involved at all?" asked Lulu as a thought occurred to her. "What if he thought that John and Dawn were in on it together—collaborating the way that John had wanted them to? Then maybe Finn kills John for revenge—trying to pay him back for murdering his father."

Cherry and Lulu sipped their drinks for a minute, mulling this over.

"But then, what about you?" asked Cherry. "Y'all get along fine. Why would he do something like that to you?"

"I don't know. I really can't believe he'd be involved in all this. He seems like a nice kid who has had a real rough time in his life. Like he wants to play music and not have his mom work too hard. He wants a normal life. It's hard to picture him as some kind of homicidal maniac who attacks old ladies in the street," said Lulu.

"Sixty is the new fifty," said Cherry. "You're not old and I'm not, either. Maybe Finn did it out of desperation . . . you know. That wouldn't make it so bad."

"What if it wasn't Finn, though?" said Lulu. "Right now, I want to think about other possibilities. Finn is only now coming out of his shell and starting to enjoy the big, wonderful world and I hate the thought of him having that ended by going to jail. Let's see. What about his mama?"

"Or," said Cherry, snapping her fingers. "What if Finn did kill Reuben? Finn had the opportunity and he'd been brainwashed for the last couple of years by his mom's bitterness. What if Finn killed Reuben and then John found out about it and *Dawn* killed John? Maybe John came to talk to Dawn again to tell her that he'd seen Finn that night and wanted to know what they should do about it. Who knows, maybe John was trying to extort money out of Dawn for keeping quiet—he did need the cash, after all."

"And Dawn was trying to make sure that no one

would find out what Finn had done," said Lulu. "So she decided to murder John to keep him quiet and to keep Finn out of jail."

"You did hear the same sound that Dawn's cell phone makes right when you were being attacked," said Cherry. "And I get the feeling that Dawn knew that you'd been nosing around in this case and might be getting close to the truth. So she decided to give you a huge scare."

"It could have happened that way," said Lulu with a sigh. "But it might not have. I wonder if the fact that I don't like Dawn very much has anything to do with the fact that I've helped you come up with a solution where she's responsible for one of the murders and behind the attack on me, too."

"She acts ugly sometimes, doesn't she?" said Cherry with a snort. "Some folks get *better* as they get older and some get *bitter*. She's a bitter one, for sure."

"Well, she does have a lot to be unhappy about," said Lulu. "Her husband treated her like crud."

"Toward the end of their marriage. But I got the impression that they got along pretty well together for years. Until his sudden, overnight change," said Cherry.

"Which had to do with the night that Tim and Reuben went out," said Lulu. "Clearly the guilt from that night really messed him up." She hesitated. "I hate to think that Tim had anything to do with this. He really seems like he's getting his life back together. And Ben told me he did a great job in the kitchen today . . . he's pleased that he's found another cook so easily."

"And why would we think Tim did it again?" asked Cherry, delicately scratching the bridge of her nose, then making a face when she ended up with green goo on her finger. "I thought he was trying to convince Reuben that they needed to come clean, pay their debt to society, and start a new life."

"Maybe Reuben tried attacking Tim," suggested Lulu.

Cherry snapped her fingers, unknowingly spreading the oatmeal goo to other fingers. "I can believe that. Heck, *I* was even fighting with Reuben that day. That guy sure was belligerent. He could have started something with Tim, trying to convince him not to talk to the police."

"Then Tim could have fought back and maybe even accidentally killed Reuben," said Lulu. "But he was so upset over the hit-and-run. It seems like he'd be even more devastated if he'd been responsible for the death of a person who used to be his close friend."

"But Reuben was a bad guy," said Cherry, pursing her lips as if tasting something sour. "It stands to reason that Tim wouldn't feel too bad about killing him. I bet he'd feel sorry about it, but if he was defending himself, he might not even feel all that responsible."

"You're probably right," said Lulu thoughtfully. "It

wouldn't be the same thing as running down an innocent person on the street."

"Or sidewalk," said Cherry.

"But can you see him killing John in cold blood? Or
attacking me?" asked Lulu.

"It's hard to imagine," admitted Cherry.

"What about Brody and his financial problems and
rocky past with Reuben?" asked Lulu.

"You know, it's one of those things where you wonder
if you can really know a person," said Cherry. "Just because I like Brody doesn't mean that he's not a murderer
in his free time."

"I have a hard time thinking of any of these folks as
murderers," admitted Lulu. She got up and washed out
her wineglass and put it in Cherry's dishwasher. "Thanks
for talking all this through with me. I can finally go
home and go to sleep now."

"Anytime, Lulu," said Cherry, smiling through her
green mask. "Don't worry. You'll get to the bottom of all
this. You always do." She added quickly, "With the help
of the best sidekick in Memphis, of course."

Chapter
16

"Don't y'all think Derrick has been acting funny?" Lulu asked Morty, Big Ben, and Buddy. It was the following afternoon and she'd actually ended up with a good night's sleep after hashing things over with Cherry. She'd pitched in and waited tables for the lunch crowd since Tim was still helping Ben back in the kitchen and one of the waitresses was out sick. Now she was enjoying time on the front porch with her friends.

"You're wondering about this again?" asked Morty. "I thought I already gave my opinion on this."

"Funny for a regular person, or funny for a teenager?" asked Buddy.

"Well, I guess funny for a teenager," said Lulu.

"Naw. It's all hormonal. Are you talking about when he came in from school a little while ago?" asked Buddy.

"Yes. He acted different, I thought," said Lulu.

Morty drawled, "He greeted us all and smiled. That's really all you can ask for from a teenager."

"I think that's real good for a teenager," said Buddy.

"Y'all are mumbling again!" bellowed Big Ben, who'd apparently forgotten his hearing aid once again. "Speak up!"

It was a good thing that Derrick had quickly disappeared into the office because they all yelled at Big Ben to fill him in.

"He's got a secret," said Big Ben in his booming voice.

"What's the secret?" asked Lulu.

"If we knew, it wouldn't be a secret," explained Big Ben loudly.

Lulu said, "I hope he's not getting into any trouble. Everything has been looking up lately. He's dating that sweet Peaches and he's helping us with our restaurant website and social media stuff that always gives me such a headache. And I thought he was done with his old friends and was hanging out with a nice group of kids."

Morty said, "Well, we know he's making new friends, too." Lulu studied him questioningly and he said, "You know—Finn. He's hanging out with Finn some, too."

Of course, she'd been debating last night whether Finn might be a murderer. She sure hoped this case was going to wind up soon. She hated wondering if people might be killers.

"Speaking of, did you get my friend's jacket back to him last night?" asked Morty.

Lulu made a face. "I did. But then I had a little scare while I was doing it." She told her friends about the cell phone ringtone.

"Lulu, I guess you know that probably half the people in Memphis have the same ringtone, right?" asked Buddy. "I actually do a bit of texting myself, since the young people like to communicate that way. So listen to this." He pulled out his phone and pushed some buttons and his phone made the same sound that she'd heard at Dawn's house.

Lulu shivered.

"It's the default ring for the phone for texts," Buddy explained.

"Or else Buddy has a secret second life as a hardened criminal," said Morty, grinning. "Do you go around mugging people at night?"

"Beats trying to get tips from playing gigs," said Buddy with a sniff. "Anyway, all I was trying to say is that it's a clue, I'll give you that. But it's not a really *specific* clue. There might be more than one suspect who has the same ringtone."

Big Ben yelled, "What are you talking about?"

"Doesn't matter," yelled back Buddy. "You don't have a cell phone!"

"So have you got any other clues?" asked Morty. "Something a little better?"

"Well, Tim did tell me yesterday, right here on this porch, that he noticed Brody's truck around the time that I was attacked," said Lulu, frowning.

"Now that sounds like a clue to me!" said Morty.

"What?" bellowed Big Ben.

Buddy said, "It might not be much of a clue, either. Lots of people have the same truck. Did it have the same tags?"

"Apparently, it's a real distinctive truck," said Lulu with a shrug. "Tim seemed pretty sure it was Brody's."

"Mumbles and mutters!" yelled Big Ben.

"Lulu said that Brody's truck was seen around the time she was attacked!" said Morty loudly, enunciating the words carefully.

Lulu caught a glimpse of something out of the corner of her eye and quickly put her finger to her lips. It was Brody, coming through the porch door. They all froze, staring at him, but Brody was determined to act normal and as if he hadn't heard anything. If he hadn't heard them talking about seeing his truck, though, then he was even deafer than Big Ben.

"How are you doing today, Brody?" asked Lulu. "Are you here to eat or to visit?"

"I'm actually a customer today. Sharon seemed kind of tired this afternoon and didn't look like she was up to doing any cooking, so I thought I'd run by and pick up supper for both of us," said Brody.

"I guess it's pretty tiring, being in charge of an estate like that," said Lulu.

"Yes, and we've got to try to figure out what to do with the stuff in his house. We're going to have to get Finn and Dawn over there to see if they want any of those things. Maybe Finn can wear some of Reuben's clothes, but I kind of doubt it. Sharon and I went through some of the stuff yesterday—things we didn't think anybody would want. It's a lot of work. No wonder she's so tired out. And of course the police keep talking to us," said Brody. "Just trying to do their jobs, but it's exhausting, too."

He talked to them a few minutes before going inside the dining room to pick up his take-out order.

"Whew!" said Buddy. "That was close!"

"Oh, he heard us talking," said Lulu. "He must have."

"I wouldn't think a thing of it," said Morty. "I bet you anything that he and Sharon are doing the same kind of talking about all the suspects in these murders, too."

"Except the suspects aren't around them when they are," said Lulu with a sigh. The dining room door opened again and this time Derrick came out, holding a paper in his hands. "Everything okay, sweetie pie?"

"I had something I wanted to show you guys," said Derrick, clearing his throat, both nervous and excited at the same time. "I got Uncle Ben and Aunt Sara to come out, too, since things are pretty slow right now in the dining room."

Ben came out on the porch, wiping his hands on his apron, and Sara hurried out behind him, still clutching a pencil and order pad. "What's going on?" asked Ben, concerned.

"Well, y'all might have noticed that I was spending a lot of time with Peaches lately," said Derrick.

Lulu really, really hoped that there wasn't going to be an announcement of impending nuptials between the two seventeen-year-olds. Peaches was as cute as a button, but her grandmama would have both their heads on platters if they decided they were going to get married.

"Peaches is really good in school, you know. And I haven't really been," said Derrick, coloring in a splotchy way.

Derrick's grades had been pretty low since he moved to Memphis. But with all the upheaval in his young life, they'd all found it completely understandable. He'd also been showing real improvement and was putting time into his studying. The problem was that he'd had a good deal of catching up to do from the years in New York, where academics weren't exactly at the forefront and making some semblance of normalcy in his mother's dysfunctional home was. The focus had been more on survival.

"So I decided that I wanted to make a real push this semester and go all out. Try to show colleges that I could be serious and I could show improvement," said Derrick.

"I've been meeting Peaches for months now, studying in the library or in the coffee shop together. And here's my report card." He shyly pulled it out.

Ben and Sara peered at it and then Ben held it up for everyone to see. "All A's!" he said with a whoop. Sara hugged Derrick tightly around his neck until Lulu wondered if the poor boy could breathe.

"So you've been studying with Peaches?" asked Lulu.

"More than studying," said Derrick. "She was tutoring me, too. Getting me caught up with everybody else."

"Why didn't you tell us?" asked Sara.

"Well, I didn't want to let you know what I was doing, in case I really bombed," said Derrick with an attempt at a careless shrug. The insecurity still showed on his face, though. He didn't want them all to be looking forward to a great report card if there was a chance that he might end up with bad grades and disappoint everybody.

Lulu reached out and gave Derrick a big hug. "I'm so proud of you, sweetie. I know you were taking tough classes, too. This calls for a celebration."

Morty snapped his fingers. "I know just the thing. The Back Porch Blues Band will play tonight in celebration of our young scholar. Derrick, I know you're a fan."

Derrick grinned at them as the men started making plans.

"I bet Finn would like to hear y'all sing and celebrate, too," said Lulu. "Why don't you give him a call and tell him to come on over tonight."

Derrick grinned even wider.

Ben said, "I'll cook up some special stuff on the grill just for Derrick. I know you especially like grilled shrimp, Derrick. And Peaches will have to be our guest of honor, since she was the tutor extraordinaire. Her food will be on the house tonight!"

Derrick gave a whoop. Lulu had the feeling that there would be many good grades in Derrick's future. Between their reaction and his own pleasure at doing well (and the boost in his self-confidence), it seemed like he was finally starting to make his peace with school.

They'd decided that the celebration would start at seven thirty that night, and once they'd settled on a time, Lulu headed home to put her feet up for a few hours.

Before she left for home, she remembered to ask Derrick to show her how to text. He was still on cloud nine with all the praise.

"It's not so hard," he said. He showed her which icon to press and how to open a new message and type in the contact name or phone number she wanted to reach.

"Where is the keyboard?" asked Lulu, frowning at the device.

"It's right here," said Derrick. He pointed at the tiny cell phone screen.

"Mercy! You mean I don't have any raised buttons to type on?" asked Lulu.

"Not on this phone. But it's okay—you'll get used to it," Derrick said in a comforting voice.

"But I've got such chubby fingers!" Lulu said, studying her hands in dismay. "How am I going to be able to make out the different letters?"

"Why don't you try to send a test message to my phone and see how you do," said Derrick.

Lulu took the phone from Derrick and stared at it in great concentration. Then she carefully followed the steps he'd shown her.

Derrick's phone beeped at him to notify him about the text and Lulu was glad that he'd chosen a different ringtone than Dawn and Sharon had. He opened the text. "Okay. So . . . *rsty mradagr.*" His brow furrowed. "I'm sure there's a message in those letters somewhere."

Lulu sighed. "It was supposed to say *test message.*"

Derrick smiled at her. "It takes time, Granny Lulu. Don't worry—before long, you'll be texting like a pro."

Back home, Lulu put her feet up for a while and was surprised to find herself waking up from a nap. She must have been more worn out than she'd thought. Glancing at the clock, she decided to head back over to the restaurant to help prepare for Derrick's big celebration. She was picking up her big key ring when her doorbell rang. She peeked out the window and saw Sharon.

This time Sharon wasn't crying, but her eyes were red like she'd been crying recently, and there was a streak of mascara on her cheek. She remembered Pink's warning from last night not to trust anybody. Could you really live your life like that, though? Lulu wasn't sure she wanted to. But she didn't want to be stupid, either. She hurried to the junk drawer in a nearby end table and pulled out a screwdriver. She could defend herself with it, although she didn't want to have to get to that point. Then she opened the door and invited Sharon to come inside and to sit down on the sofa with her.

Sharon said, "Lulu, I hope you don't mind that I dropped by. I called the restaurant this morning and they said that you hadn't come in yet. There was something I wanted to talk to you about." She frowned, studying the bruises on Lulu's arms from the fall. "Is something wrong? Has something happened?"

"Oh, I'm fine. But I had an incident when I was leaving the restaurant last night." She told Sharon what had happened.

Sharon's reaction to the story was pretty strong. Her eyes widened and she gasped when she heard the news. "And this was last night? When?"

Lulu said, "Around midnight probably. I sort of lost track of time last night."

Sharon slumped into the sofa, buried her face in her hands, and groaned.

"Sharon? What is it?" asked Lulu.

Sharon lifted her head. "It might be nothing," she said in a tone that sounded like she was trying to reason with herself as much as with Lulu. Then she shook her head. "No, it's definitely something. It shows me how bad everything really is."

She gave Lulu a weak smile. "You must think I'm a nut. I've always got drama going on. But what I'm trying to figure out right now is why Brody was out last night around midnight."

Lulu's heart skipped a beat. "Oh." So Tim had definitely seen Brody's truck. Her mind spun trying to find a reasonable explanation for him to have been in the parking deck. She couldn't come up with one.

"Yeah. But Lulu, I can't imagine Brody hurting you. He told me how much he enjoyed meeting you and how great you were. I can't believe I'm even talking like this. Brody couldn't hurt anybody. He's not that kind of a person. Not the sweet guy that I fell in love with."

"Where did he say he was last night?" asked Lulu.

"He said something about going to the store . . . that he'd forgotten that he'd run out of toiletries that he needed for getting ready for work," said Sharon.

"Did he come back home with toiletries?" asked Lulu.

"He did. But when I checked under the bathroom sink, there were still plenty of deodorants and toothpastes and stuff like that under there," said Sharon. "Besides, he was gone for a long time. He could have gone over to Aunt Pat's, attacked you, then run by the store on the way back home." She stopped. "No, I don't believe it. He couldn't have done it."

Lulu said, "Y'all have been married a long while, haven't you? Does that seem like the kind of thing that Brody could possibly have done?"

Sharon dropped her gaze. "I have a tough time wrapping my head around the idea that he could have done something like that. I mean, yes, he's had minor scrapes with the law before. We've been married for about ten years, but before we were married, he was doing some things that I wasn't happy about. He hung out with a kind of wild crowd of people for one—and went to parties where sometimes there were people there doing drugs. He wasn't one of the druggies . . . but because he was there, sometimes he'd get in trouble, too. But the way he was with me was always so gentle—so sweet."

"He's stayed out of trouble since y'all have been married?" asked Lulu.

"For the most part. One time he got arrested for gambling, but that was it. Besides, he knew I don't like gambling, so he made sure he stopped. And he had a DUI once. That was all," said Sharon.

It sounded like a lot to Lulu. But then, she'd led a pretty sheltered life.

"Sharon," said Lulu slowly. "You didn't know about last night when you came over here. Why did you visit?"

Now Sharon appeared even more deflated until Lulu had to wonder if she was going to disappear completely into the stuffing of her sofa. "I came because I wanted to talk to you about the night that John died."

Lulu leaned forward.

"You see," said Sharon with a sigh. "Brody had gone out that night. He'd told me that he'd wanted to blow off steam. Everything had been so stressful with Reuben acting so weird and then being murdered. Even our being the will executors was making us stressed out. He'd met this guy named Jim at work and he'd gone out a couple of times with him after work. Once I'd joined them and Jim's wife had, too."

Lulu nodded.

"So I told him sure. I told him to go on out and have a nice time with Jim. I was worn out that night and I was in the bed by nine o'clock. I woke up when he came back in—it was probably around eleven thirty, which I thought was pretty late. But I was still so exhausted that I fell back asleep right away," said Sharon.

"Then, of course, the next morning I discovered John's body and was a total wreck. I've been trying to cope with all this since I found John. But yesterday, I ran into Jim's wife at the grocery store. I asked her if Jim and Brody had a nice dinner the other night. She looked at me real funny and said that Jim hadn't been out with anybody for the whole last week—Jim's mother has been in the hospital and his sister was staying with them and they were at the hospital all the time." Sharon stared at Lulu with a bewildered expression on her face.

Lulu took a deep breath. "What do you think he was actually doing?"

Sharon gave a brittle laugh and started working on picking off her nail polish again. "I don't know. When I came over here to tell you about it, it's because I needed a sounding board. I figured that Brody was seeing another woman or something like that. And that made me upset. I hated thinking that he might be cheating on me. But what if he isn't? Now that I've spoken to you and I know he was out when you were attacked last night, it makes me wonder if maybe he was out murdering John instead of being with a woman."

Lulu sat in silence for a moment. Brody seemed like a nice guy, but his lack of alibi was disturbing. Plus the fact that Tim had spotted Brody with a tarp shortly before Reuben was murdered. Pink told her that Brody and Sharon were in deep financial trouble. It sure did seem awfully convenient that now they had enough money to take care of all their money problems.

Lulu said, "Honey, you need to ask Brody about where he's been. Maybe there's a perfectly good explanation. If you let your suspicions run rampant, then things are only going to get worse."

Sharon groaned. "I don't know if I can ask him. I dread his answer too much. Can you come with me when I ask him? Because, what if he *is* a murderer and he killed Reuben for the money and then killed John to cover it all up? If he knows that I know, maybe he'll kill me, too."

Chapter

17

"Of course I'll come with you," said Lulu stoutly. "Although I don't think you have a thing to worry about."

But she patted the screwdriver in her dress pocket. Just to make sure it was still there.

"Do you want me to drive or do you want to drive?" asked Sharon. "Oh wait. I'm blocking you. So I'll drive and I can bring you back."

Lulu was thinking about Derrick's celebration. She really didn't want to miss out showing him support and cheering him on. But maybe this wouldn't take all that long. Or maybe it would get ugly—if Brody had killed two people, what might happen? Pink's warning about keeping safe was really ringing in her ears.

"That sounds good, Sharon. I'm going to run to the little girls' room real quick before we go," said Lulu.

As soon as she got back to her bedroom and bathroom, Lulu pulled out her cell phone. Texting when she was in a hurry was going to be interesting. She felt so flustered that she could barely remember how to do it. She pushed the icon for texting, then peered at the contacts. She sent a message to Derrick that said she would be running late, but sent kisses and hugs. Except it looked more like *runinf laat. Kises abd hygs.*

Then she decided she better cover her bases. What if Brody started acting crazy? Would Sharon and Lulu be able to handle him? Should they? But maybe he wasn't even the person responsible for all this. So she sent another text—this one to Cherry. It said that she and Sharon were going to talk to Brody—Sharon suspected he might be involved in the murders. Except the text, of course, was more like *Shron snf i goingtakk to Brody. Might br invokvrd.*

This texting wasn't so bad, really. The nice thing was that she didn't have to have a phone conversation that would make Sharon think that Lulu believed Brody was guilty. That would make Sharon probably burst into hysterical tears at a point where it was much better for her to be cool and collected and approach Brody in a firm and logical manner. With texting, she hadn't had to say a word.

Lulu turned off the volume on her phone. She didn't need to be talking to Brody and have text messages popping up all over the place. She put it in her pocketbook and joined Sharon. "You remember Derrick, don't you? We're having a little party for him tonight at Aunt Pat's to celebrate his all-A report card," said Lulu.

Sharon smiled at him, more relaxed than she had a few minutes ago. "Are you? That's great. He seems like a really nice kid."

"He is. He's had a rough time in school, and a report card like this one goes to show how much work he's put into his studying," said Lulu.

"Am I going to mess you up, then?" asked Sharon with an anxious frown. "I don't want to make it so that you can't get back to Aunt Pat's in time for Derrick's party."

"We'll be good," said Lulu. "I'm sure this conversation won't take all that long."

They climbed into Sharon's car and took off. Sharon seemed mighty nervous. She sighed. "I sure do miss smoking. I used to love me a cigarette when I got this jittery. Took the edge right off. But I quit a few years back and I know it would be a slippery slope if I even had one."

"Are you having a bad gut feeling about this?" asked Lulu. "I know you're nervous about talking to Brody about his whereabouts—is that what's making you feel this anxious? Do you think he's going to lash out at you or anything?" Or lash out at *us*?

Sharon gave a laugh that she probably hoped sounded light. "Oh no, I can't imagine Brody doing something like that. But I don't know what he's going to say when I ask him about it. It's the not knowing that makes me worried."

Sharon was clearly trying to stay distracted and asked Lulu to tell her more about Derrick and where he'd come from. "He's not your grandchild, is he?"

"Technically? No, he's not. But I've sort of adopted him as my grandson. He's my daughter-in-law's nephew." She explained how Derrick had come to them and the situation he'd left and how far he'd come. The pride might have leaked into her voice, but she couldn't help it—Sara and Ben had done a great thing rescuing that boy from his home, and Derrick had done a great job working as hard as he had. She really thought he had a bright future ahead of him.

Lulu was so carried away with telling the story and Sharon seemed like such a rapt audience that it took a while for Lulu to notice that they weren't going to Brody and Sharon's house. "Aren't we going to your house?"

"Brody isn't there," sighed Sharon. "Which is what gave me so much time to think today. He's at a restaurant—he decided to eat out after work. So we'll meet up with him then, if that's okay?"

Lulu thought again about the celebratory meal going on at Aunt Pat's. But there was something else that was bothering her. She replayed their conversation for the last few minutes in her head, frowning.

Finally, she knew what it was and a cold chill crept up her spine. Why would Brody have gone to a restaurant after work when he'd picked up a large to-go order from Aunt Pat's for both of them only this afternoon?

She tried to keep calm and pressed the palms of her hands against her floral dress. She said in what she hoped was a careless voice, "This is a nice car, Sharon. Is this the one you usually drive?"

"Most of the time," she said in a distracted tone. "Except when Brody has to drive clients around at work, then he takes this one and I drive his truck."

"That's right, he works at the bank, doesn't he? Does he have to drive clients around fairly often?" asked Lulu, still trying to sound offhand as if she were only making conversation.

Sharon's cell phone made a cheerful chirp. Lulu's breath caught.

Sharon ignored the incoming text, but her eyes narrowed and her fingers gripped the steering wheel a little tighter. "Why so many questions about the car, Lulu? Wouldn't have anything to do with the fact that you saw Brody's truck the other night, would it?"

Lulu just stared at her, eyes wide.

"Oh, come on, did you think Brody wasn't going to tell me the fact that he overheard you saying you'd seen his truck the night you were attacked?" said Sharon in a hard voice.

Lulu said, "But I *didn't* see it. Tim saw it. And it wasn't only me he told."

Sharon was barely listening. "The problem is, Lulu,

that you know something. I don't know exactly what and I don't know how. But I can't let you tell Pink," said Sharon, an icy edge to her voice.

"Sharon, I don't know what you're talking about. I thought you and I were going to ask Brody where he's been lately," said Lulu, still thinking that she might be able to get out of the situation if she didn't acknowledge what was really happening.

Sharon's eyes watched the road as she drove farther out of town. "No. You know that's not where we're going," she said tersely.

"You're the one who murdered Reuben and John," said Lulu in a heavy voice. "Why, Sharon? Was it because you needed the money?"

"Of course I needed the money. There was never a time when I didn't need the money," she snapped. "Even when I thought that Brody and I were doing okay, we weren't in good shape. The last couple of months I've been thinking that we're going to lose our house, our stuff—everything that we've worked for. And Reuben always ran his mouth about how much money he had. He bragged all the time. One day he'd been drinking and told me that he was getting back at his ex-wife by changing his will in favor of Brody and me. That made everything a lot clearer for me."

"Did Brody know what you were doing?" asked Lulu.

"Of course not," said Sharon in a scornful tone. "Brody doesn't have the guts to do something like that and he always had a soft spot for Reuben. Why, I don't know. If I'd let Brody know what I'd done, he would have acted so guilty that everybody would have known. The man can't keep a secret to save his life."

"Why did you kill John?" asked Lulu. "Was it because he knew you'd murdered Reuben?" Lulu was now making sure she knew where the locks and door handle were on Sharon's car in case she had an opportunity to try to escape.

"John had seen me struggling with Reuben," said Sharon. "Or he saw me take the tarp from Brody and figured out the rest—I'm not sure which. The problem is that he thought he could make some kind of deal with me. He needed money, too, and he planned on blackmailing me so that he could finally hire a contractor to finish the mess his house was in. Too bad for him that he didn't realize I wasn't the blackmailing type."

"So you killed John, left, and came back again later to 'discover' the body," said Lulu.

"I figured that finding the body and being upset by discovering it would help give me believability," said Sharon with a shrug of one shoulder.

"And you attacked me when I was leaving Aunt Pat's," said Lulu.

"Don't take it personally," said Sharon, emotionlessly glancing at her before focusing back at the road. "I was trying to keep you from being nosy. It obviously didn't work, though, so I'm moving on to plan B."

Lulu's thoughts whirled. She thought about trying to text Cherry again, but how would Cherry find her way out here? And Sharon would see what she was doing anyway. She wiped her sweaty palms on her dress again and this time her hand brushed over the screwdriver in her pocket. She also realized that basically she was allowing Sharon to drive her to what was going to become a crime scene—with Lulu as the victim.

She also saw that there was a yard that had a really generous number of large wax myrtle bushes in the backyard. And that they weren't going very fast. Lulu took a deep breath, and said quickly, "What's that over there?"

Sharon turned to look through her window and Lulu grabbed the steering wheel, yanking it as hard as she could into the bushes. Sharon shrieked and slammed on the brakes, which squealed and shuddered in protest. The impact with the bushes was enough to shake them up but didn't hurt them. That's when Lulu decided it was time to get out of Sharon's car. She pulled off her seat belt, hit the unlock button, jumped out, and ran to the nearest house and pounded on the door, glancing fearfully behind her as she knocked.

Nobody immediately answered and she couldn't hear anyone inside the house—and a furious Sharon was rocketing out of her car in pursuit. And she was a much younger woman than Lulu.

Lulu tried the doorknob to see if the door was open.

It was. She fumbled to open the door, then shut it, hard, and—hands shaking—slid the chain on. Sharon yelled and threw herself at the door, pounding on it, and pushed the door as far as it would go with the chain on.

Now there was movement behind Lulu and a low growling. Desperately, she turned around . . . and saw a German shepherd almost as big as the small room she was standing in. She froze. She started reaching for the screwdriver again, then hesitated and realized that old habits die hard and she actually had that huge pocketbook of hers dangling daintily from her arm in this life-and-death struggle. She slowly put her hand in the bag and rummaged around gently.

Her hand closed around it . . . the jar of peanut butter she'd finally remembered to bring for the office break room for Coco. The dog's teeth were bared now and the growling louder. Nothing to put the peanut butter on . . . wait. She stuck her hand in her purse again and pulled out the zipper bag of treats for the Labs. She tossed one treat, plain, to the German shepherd, then dipped two others in the peanut butter and tossed them away from her toward the back of the house—where she was hearing somebody coming in through the back door.

Sharon.

Lulu waited until Sharon was several paces into the house, then slid off the chain and ran through the front door to the car. Surely Sharon hadn't had the presence of mind to lock the doors of the car.

They were unlocked. Better yet, the key was still in the ignition.

Lulu turned the key, and the car started up as Sharon bolted, wild-eyed, from the front door of the little house, the German shepherd tearing after her as she shoved at the animal's head and tried to shut the front door closed. Lulu didn't wait to see if Sharon succeeded—she threw the car into reverse, floored the accelerator, and took off.

This worked out real well until Sharon's car decided to die from whatever injuries it had sustained from its hard landing in the bushes. Lulu was over a block away but still in full view of Sharon.

For the first time in her cell phone ownership, she was grateful to hear the usually annoying sound of the ringtone. She quickly answered it.

"Cherry?" she gasped. "Is that you?"

"It's Pink, Lulu. Cherry called me because you'd texted her something real garbled and you hadn't shown up at Derrick's party. Where are you?"

"Pink, I don't know exactly where I am. I'm somewhere kind of remote, probably right outside the city," said Lulu. "And Sharon is the one behind all this, Pink. She drove me out here to kill me and I'm in her car right now. It's stalled out and she's coming back after me."

Pink's voice was alert but very calm. "Okay, Lulu. Can you see a street sign or anything that can help me find you? And can you describe Sharon's car? I'm driving around now and I'll try to get to you as fast as I can."

Lulu squinted in front of her, but the nearest street sign was blurry. "I can't quite make it out." Then she turned around and she could make out the next sign, behind her. "I can see the one behind me, though. It's Trellis Lane." She described Sharon's sedan to Pink.

"I'm on my way," he said.

Sharon ran toward her. Lulu hit the locks again, just to make sure. "She's coming my way, Pink. And she has a knife in her hand."

"Are your doors locked? Do you have anything that you can use as a weapon, if you need to?"

Lulu said, "I grabbed a screwdriver before I left my house. I sure would hate to use it, but believe me, if it's me or her, I'll make sure I use the thing."

"I don't think she's going to get very far using a knife on a car," said Pink dryly. "But if she starts using her head and finds something to smash in your window, you need to be ready."

Lulu took a deep breath as Sharon finally reached the car and launched herself at it, beating it with her palms. "I think she's really disturbed, Pink."

"Hang in there, Lulu."

Chapter

18

Sharon's face was so furious and her features were so distorted that Lulu turned away. Lulu noticed that Sharon was getting some attention from the neighbors, who were at their windows and in their doorways, watching her.

It wouldn't hurt to have more witnesses, right? Lulu blared on the horn in long blasts, which brought more curious people from other houses out. And that made Sharon very, very mad.

Sharon started hitting the car with the knife—slashing the tires and cutting the paint as she swiped at the hood. And she didn't stop yelling, although it was hard to tell exactly what she was saying.

When the police cars arrived, Lulu saw that none of

them contained Pink—the neighbors must have called 911 and the closest officers responded. Sharon seemed to not even register their presence . . . until they handcuffed her and put her in the back of a police car.

Unfortunately, Lulu was also detained for a while. But then, she'd been sitting there in a damaged car that didn't belong to her. Once Pink arrived, he set everything straight. And he made sure that Lulu was taken home—the celebration for Derrick had already wound down and Lulu needed time to recover from her wild ride with Sharon.

It was hours later before Pink checked back in with her. It was real late and Lulu had been thinking about going to bed. She'd been descended upon by an indignant and loving horde of family and Graces and Morty, who'd demanded to know if she was all right, fussed at her for riding off with Sharon, and admired her for getting out of the situation alive.

Now they'd all left, shaking their heads. Except for Cherry, and Lulu was seriously considering pressuring her to take her leave, too. Once the doorbell rang and they saw that it was Pink, Lulu knew she'd have Cherry as a visitor for a while longer.

Cherry was breathless and didn't wait for Pink to even sit down before she started giving him the fifth degree. "Did y'all get anything out of her, Pink? I bet she clammed up real quick, didn't she? Think she's going to get away with it all?"

Lulu sighed. "There really wasn't any evidence, was there? I don't think you can convict anybody because their husband picked up take-out instead of going to a restaurant."

Pink laughed. "Well, y'all are wrong. We read Sharon her rights and she decided to spill everything. It was like a dam bursting and she couldn't keep it all in. We even repeated a mention of a lawyer, worried that her confession wasn't going to count in court—but she kept right on talking. Couldn't wait to get it off her chest."

"What a relief!" said Lulu. "I was thinking it was going to be my word against hers."

"Of course, there were a ton of onlookers who could have backed you up on how she was trying to attack you, Lulu. Y'all did draw a lot of attention," said Pink. "That was probably the excitement of the year for those folks."

"Good entertainment value," said Cherry, chortling. "Although I don't know why I'm laughing. I'm still so mad at Sharon that I could spit. She tricked us into being her friend! She acted so . . . damaged. I thought she was a good person."

"She was a good actress," said Lulu. She thought for a moment. "Sharon said that Brody wasn't part of the scheme. Is that what she told y'all, too?"

"He sure seemed surprised when we paid a visit on him tonight," said Pink. "He'd been texting Sharon trying to figure out where she was. So apparently he didn't know anything about her plan to get rid of Lulu. And he claims not to know anything about Reuben's murder or John's."

"The motivation was money, obviously," said Cherry.

"That's what Sharon said. Their whole lifestyle was endangered and Reuben bragged that he had more money than he actually did. And apparently Reuben and Sharon were a lot closer than we realized. They started an affair shortly after Sharon and Brody moved to Memphis. Reuben was drunk one day and told Sharon he'd changed his will and was leaving nearly everything to her and Brody. He didn't know how desperate they were or that Sharon would now have a motive to kill him."

"I'm surprised she could take down a big guy like Reuben with a knife," said Cherry.

"Not me!" said Lulu. "She was strong as an ox."

"She seemed real focused and determined," said Pink. "And that desperation of hers drove her pretty hard, too. It might have made her even stronger than she was."

"Did y'all hear anything from the people whose house I broke into?" asked Lulu.

"Lulu the burglar," chortled Cherry.

Pink said, "Technically, you didn't break into the house since the door was unlocked. It was more like trespassing. And no, they didn't seem to mind—they understood why you came inside. Although their bushes have now got to be seriously pruned. And they did say their dog has an upset tummy."

Lulu said, "Poor thing. I know I scooped out too much, but I was in a hurry."

"It was quick thinking, though," said Pink admiringly. "You really got yourself out of a pickle."

"I have you to thank for that, Pink," said Lulu. "You're the one who told me to stay alert and be prepared to fight."

"It was real gutsy of you to plow the car into the bushes," said Cherry.

"Better than going off with a killer to a remote location," said Pink. "But I do think it was very brave of you."

"And I won't say anything again about the fact that you tote that huge pocketbook," said Cherry. "Or the fact that it's always on your arm." She looked pointedly at Lulu, and sure enough, the purse nestled in the crook of her arm.

"I'm thinking that even if she's not pulling out survival gear from that pocketbook, it could be a weapon all by itself," mused Pink. "Just seeing the size of it and the probable weight."

"There was probably a time in my life when I could have put all my stuff in a tee-tiny pocketbook," said Lulu. Then she stopped, thinking. "No, actually, likely not. I've always toted most of my stuff with me."

"I'm glad you do," said Cherry. "Who knows when we might need something from the Pocketbook of Power the next time we have an adventure?"

Recipes

Pineapple Casserole

1 20-ounce can pineapple chunks
1 cup sugar
4 tablespoons flour
1 cup grated cheddar cheese
1 stick melted margarine
1 cup crushed buttery crackers

Preheat the oven to 350 degrees.

Drain most of the juice from the canned pineapple (leave about 6 tablespoons), and pour the chunks and remaining juice into a casserole dish.

Mix the sugar and flour, and pour the mixture on top of the pineapple chunks.

Sprinkle the cheese on the top.

Mix the melted margarine and crushed crackers together and sprinkle on the top of the cheese.

Bake for 30 minutes.

◇◇◇◇◇◇◇◇◇

Simply Southern Pimento Cheese

8 ounces of extra-sharp cheddar cheese, cubed

1 4-ounce jar pimentos, with liquid

1 cup mayonnaise

1 squirt regular mustard

1 dash garlic powder

Put all the ingredients in a blender. Blend until smooth. Refrigerate for about 45 minutes for the pimento cheese to thicken into a spread.

◇◇◇◇◇◇◇◇◇

Bread Pudding

2 eggs, slightly beaten
2¼ cups milk
1 teaspoon vanilla
½ teaspoon ground cinnamon
¼ teaspoon salt
2 cups day-old bread, cut into 1-inch cubes
½ cup brown sugar
½ cup raisins
¼ cup butter
½ cup caramel topping
vanilla ice cream (if desired)

Preheat the oven to 350 degrees. Combine the eggs, milk, vanilla, cinnamon, and salt. Stir in the bread, brown sugar, and raisins. Pour into an 8-inch round baking pan and dot with butter. Put the baking pan inside a larger pan containing an inch of water. Bake for 30 minutes. Remove from the oven and top with caramel and vanilla ice cream.

◇◇◇◇◇◇◇◇◇

Three-Bean Casserole

1 package frozen French-style green beans

1 package frozen lima beans

1 package frozen baby green peas

1 tablespoon mayonnaise

1½ cups sour cream

3 ounces softened cream cheese

1 medium onion, finely chopped

salt and pepper to taste

1 can drained and sliced water chestnuts (optional)

1 tablespoon lemon juice

¼ tablespoon Worcestershire sauce

1 cup shredded Parmesan cheese

dash of paprika

Preheat the oven to 350 degrees. Cook the beans and peas according to directions. Drain and place in a greased casserole dish. Combine the mayonnaise, sour cream, cream cheese, onion, salt and pepper, and water chestnuts (if desired) and add to the bean mixture. Mix the lemon juice and Worcestershire sauce and add to other ingredients. Sprinkle the Parmesan cheese and paprika on top. Bake for 30 minutes.

◇◇◇◇◇◇◇◇◇

Blueberry Muffins

¼ cup vegetable oil

½ cup sugar

2 eggs

⅔ cup milk

2 tablespoons boiling water

1 teaspoon vanilla

½ teaspoon almond extract

1¾ cups self-rising flour

1 cup fresh or frozen blueberries

Preheat the oven to 350 degrees. Cream together the oil and sugar. Add the eggs, milk, and water and beat together. Add the flavorings. Add the flour and beat at a low speed until mixed. Fold in the blueberries. Fill greased muffin cups two-thirds of the way full, distributing the berries evenly. Bake for 20–25 minutes or until turning brown.

◇◇◇◇◇◇◇◇◇

Chocolate Chip Mini Cheesecakes

BASE

2 cups Oreo crumbs

8 tablespoons melted margarine

FILLING

2 (8-ounce) packages cream cheese, softened to room
temperature

½ cup white sugar

2 eggs

1 teaspoon vanilla extract

1½ cups mini chocolate chips

TOPPING

1½ teaspoons chocolate ganache

Preheat the oven to 350 degrees. Line mini muffin tins with mini paper liners.

Crush the Oreos and mix with the melted margarine. Put ½ teaspoon of the crushed cookie mixture into each paper cup.

In a mixing bowl, beat the softened cream cheese, gradually adding the sugar, eggs, and vanilla until the mixture is silky smooth with no lumps. Add the mini chocolate chips. Fill the paper liners nearly to the top with the mixture.

Bake for 15 minutes, and remove before the cheesecakes crack, while the centers are still soft. Cool. Top with the chocolate ganache.

◇◇◇◇◇◇◇◇◇